A Candlelight Regency Special

The Audacious Miss

Joan Vincent

A Candlelight
Regency Special

THE
AUDACIOUS MISS

Joan Vincent

A CANDLELIGHT REGENCY SPECIAL

To Patty and Clayton
for
"Joan Vincent"

Published by
Dell Publishing Co., Inc.
1 Dag Hammarskjold Plaza
New York, New York 10017

Dell ® TM 681510, Dell Publishing Co., Inc.

ISBN 0–440–10228–6

Printed in the United States of America

First printing—June 1982

CHAPTER I

"Miss Audacia." The voice commanded the slim figure clad in breeches to halt. " 'Tis no day for a young lady to be about and, as I have told you, your appearance in those . . . things is a slur on all modest women. Have you no care for what others think?"

"Oh, Miss Bea," moaned the impatient young woman, "let us not discuss Daniel's breeches again. Recall that we have an understanding that I may see to my toilet. Now, I am certain Father will be wanting tea. Mustn't make him wait," Audacia Aderly warned the spinster housekeeper.

"My, yes. Tea. Tsk, tsk. How careless of me . . . Miss Audacia, come back!" she called as the girl slipped through the doorway. "That young miss. What am I to do?" the housekeeper grumbled as she closed the door. "Why was it I ever agreed to her going about in her brother's breeches?" The tall, thin, gray-haired woman shook her head as she turned toward the kitchen. "Oh, yes. It was that vile green coil of a snake she brought from behind her back shortly after she broached the matter." Miss Bea spoke aloud, assuring herself it had not been a dreadful dream. "My, my. What shall become of her— gadding about in men's clothing, paying no mind to any of the decencies?" The worried woman looked about the kitchen. "Now why did I come here? Oh my, the tea. Sir Aderly will be upset, I fear, at having to wait. If only I could prompt him to take as much note of his daughter's behavior as of a late tea."

The crisp squeaking crunch of boots upon the January snow alerted Audacia to another's approach. Pushing the still, furry mound in her hand inside her overlarge great-coat, she cinched the belt tightly to keep the young creature safe. In the clear, cold air, the footsteps carried clearly and bespoke the imminent arrival of two men. Fearful of discovery, Audacia eased her way behind a stand of young firs.

When the men were almost upon her, they halted. "The beast has rested here," a firm, unfamiliar voice said. "It must feel safe."

"Little does it know of your tenacity," the other replied.

"Geoffrey?" The whisper escaped her before she was able to halt it. She slipped a hand among the fir branches, trying to catch a glimpse of the pair. Their conversation ended, the men strode forward briskly, certain once more of the direction taken by their quarry. As she edged from behind the firs, Audacia's searching eyes caught the musket carried by the larger man. *He promised me!* she thought angrily.

* * *

"Are your lands free of ruffians?" the larger man asked in low tones when the two halted to rest.

"Ruffians? You are not in London now. I have never had any problem . . ." The words died at his friend's signal.

"A lone man has been following us this hour past. No, do not look, his eyes watch us closely."

"How do you know this? I have seen—heard—nothing," objected the other in muted tones.

"I caught a glimpse of the fellow when he traveled parallel to us for a time. A thin fellow of medium height but garbed in a greatcoat several sizes too large for him, with the oddest purple hat pulled down over his face. He dropped back when our steps slowed."

"A greatcoat several sizes too large? A purple hat? But that would be . . . No, there are none here who have reason to hide from me. You must have imagined it." the shorter of the two dismissed the notion. "Let us go a little further and see if you cannot bring the wild dog down. I am almost as frozen now as I was on the infernal march to Corunna in aught-nine."

The other's eyes darkened with a haunted melancholy; he shifted the musket irritably. "Let's get it done then," he snapped and stalked off.

Squire Webster shrugged and frowned at his friend's reaction to his words. *'Tis I who lost the arm on that march,* he thought, *not you Roland. What torments you, saddens you?* Shaking his head, he trod after his friend, his worry for the other's state of mind increased.

The Honorable Geoffrey Webster, tall, fair-haired, with warm, intelligent eyes that emphasized his slender face, and Roland, Earl Greydon, taller still, with a black mane

7

and coffee-brown, impenetrable eyes boldly set in a strong square-featured face were long acquainted. Despite Geoffrey's being a younger son and Roland heir of the Marquess of Mandel, they had become fast friends while at Oxford. It had been a sad day for Geoffrey when school came to an end and he entered the army while Roland went home to learn the duties of his title. It was, therefore, with some surprise that Geoffrey learned that his friend had purchased a coronetcy, despite family resistance, when war was renewed in 1803. The two were one-and-twenty that year and went to war with the enthusiasm of the inexperienced.

The glory of the army was soon dimmed by the mud of Portugal, the suffering, and the endless lack of supplies. Through the hardships endured, their friendship was welded into a lasting bond.

The peninsular campaign began to fail badly after Wellesley's withdrawal as commander, and Sir John Moore was at last forced to call for retreat when he learned Napoleon himself was marching toward them. It was on the beginning of that mad retreat to Corunna that Geoffrey had been wounded. It was Roland who refused to leave him behind to the mercy of the French. He helped the surgeon remove the gangerous arm and mourned its loss as if it were his own.

Since their return to England, they had seen each other only once, for Geoffrey had returned to his estate in Warwickshire to nurse his wound and Roland had gone back to the peninsula with Wellesley and gone on until Waterloo.

Greydon sold out of the army shortly after the great battle at Waterloo and in this year of 1816 was still trying to forget the war with far less success than those who had danced their way through the Congress of Vienna.

Their chance encounter in London before Christmas had led to Roland's coming to Warwickshire for a visit.

"There." Roland dropped to a knee ahead of Geoffrey. "See the black patch?" he asked, pointing to a cluster of birch. "This shall be the end of that lamb-eater's days." The musket was raised to his shoulder and aim taken.

Geoffrey stood absolutely still, hoping the cocking of the Brown Bess would not alert the wild dog. His attention was drawn away by an angry-stepped approach from behind.

"Geoffrey Webster, you promised you wouldn't allow anyone to—No!" Audacia plunged forward, pushing Geoffrey aside and down as he tried to stop her, and tumbled against Lord Greydon just as he fired.

The wild dog rose and fled instantly. His life would have been forfeit had not the lean figure jarred Greydon at the instant he fired the musket. Flinging aside the shotpiece, his lordship lunged for the greatcoated figure as she scrambled to her feet. His free hand twisted her to face him.

Something in the angry eyes sparked a response within Audacia, but her wrath refused to acknowledge it. She lashed out at the earl's shins with her stoutly booted foot. "Release me, you oaf. Who are you to lay hold of me? Geoffrey, where are you? Tell him to release me."

"A devilishly conceited lad," Roland commented, holding his twisting, kicking handful at arm's length, "to take the liberty of using your given name. A lesson he's needing."

9

Sitting in the snow where he had fallen, Geoffrey erupted in laughter.

"The least you could do is tell me what you deem fit punishment for this miscreant," Roland demanded, irritated by his friend's mirth. "Or do you intend to do nothing?"

"Geoffrey, make this bear release me this instant," a fiery-faced Audacia demanded.

"You know the lad?" Greydon asked as his friend's humor lessened enough to allow him to rise.

"That I do. Let loose your hold, friend."

Greydon's hand let go the collar of the greatcoat, and immediately his attacker kicked him in the shins once again. With a swift move of his offended leg, he knocked the boy to his seat in the cold snow.

Great, gray eyes ablaze with anger bore into his. "You —you oaf of a bear. Why not use the musket on me?"

One of his lordship's large, gloved hands pushed the "lad" flat on his back. "Your parents did a sad job of your manners, lad. You've poor words to say after friend Webster's loss."

"Loss? That poor beast? Why I am no more able to defend myself than it," sputtered the prone figure, a prisoner of his lordship's hand.

"That poor creature," Greydon said scathingly, "was a wild dog. A lamb-eater that happens to have attacked my friend's flock." His jaw locked as he jerked upright and angrily retrieved his musket.

Open-mouthed, Audacia sat and stared after him. "Is what he says true, Geoffrey?"

"Yes, my unhesitant, daring 'friend.' How oft must you

10

be admonished to caution?" he asked, extending his hand to help the seated figure rise.

"In truth, I thought," the contrite voice began, "that is, I had heard you had a London visitor who loved to hunt and . . . well, that—that person had no reason to treat me thus."

"You are fortunate I don't warm the leather of my belt on your backside, lad," Greydon told Audacia, joining the two.

"You wouldn't dare," was thrown back haughtily.

"Geoffrey, hold this musket," Greydon said stepping forward towards the lad who was glaring a dare.

Seeing the thunderous look upon Greydon's face, Audacia backed away and finally broke into a run, escaping into the thickness of trees all about.

"Hold, Roland," Geoffrey said, his hand touching his friend's arm. "No harm or insult was meant." He broke into laughter. "If you could have but seen yourself . . ."

"The lad needs to be disciplined. Has he always been allowed to roam about interfering as he liked?"

"I imagine there are those who have tried a hand with him, but I can imagine none coming out ahead in such a confrontation." Webster studied his friend's serious frown and again burst into laughter.

"Perhaps the joke would be best shared," snapped the earl. "Do you think nothing of your 'precious' lambs?" *Or of yourself?* he thought, the shadows haunting his darkening eyes as he covertly assessed his friend for any injury from the fall; Geoffrey's pinned empty sleeve was a reminder of his debt.

"There will be another day to end the wild dog's life.

My men will be set to the task," Geoffrey said, trying to assume a more solemn expression. Slapping the earl on the back, he said, "The joke will be shared soon enough. In good time, my friend."

CHAPTER II

Panting for breath, Audacia gradually slowed to a walk, but she glanced back often for assurance she wasn't being followed.

How was I to know it was a dog gone wild and killer too, she thought through gritted teeth, angry with herself. She looked back again. Would Geoffrey let that lout follow? More to fact—Audacia made a face—could Geoffrey prevent him from it?

Trudging homeward, she continued to ponder on the man. "One of those London fops no less. He must have had twelve capes to his cloak," she sneered for lack of a better criticism. The weight of the argument was lost in view of Geoffrey's description of fops as spindly, weak dandies who were afraid of their own shadows. The feel of that hard hand pinning her to the ground denied weakness, and the square-shouldered solidity of the man disavowed any degree of paltry thinness. Audacia reluctantly admitted that, in truth, he was singularly handsome. And his reaction was certainly more defensible than her own, she thought, strangely dismayed at the impression she must have made. Though angered, he had used his strength with restraint. She would have no bruise from his grip. She absently placed her hand on the arm he had held. "Oh, why must I ever be so . . ." Audacia shook her head, her musing drifting back to the earl's strong jaw line, his firm lips.

The clang of machinery parts as she drew within sight of home distracted Audacia from her contemplation. Father is hard at work and hopefully Miss Bea has retreated to her room to be away from the "clanging clatter" as she calls it, the young woman thought. At the back of the house she slipped through a door that opened into the kitchen. After a quick glance about it, she sighed with relief and pulled the purple wool cap from her head and shook her hair free.

"Miss Bea will be ready to tar and feather you if she sees you in such a state, lass."

"Oh, Mr. Ballin. You should never do that," Audacia said, recovering from the start the small, trim Irishman had given her. Her words scolded but the look she gave was filled with relief.

"You had best re-do your hair before Miss Bea . . ."

"Mr. Ballin, who are you speaking to?" Miss Bea asked, coming into the kitchen from the central hallway. "Audacia Aderly! What on earth . . . ? Where have you been? What has happened? Oh, I knew gadding about in those horrible breeches would be the end of you," the housekeeper wailed.

"Come now, woman, calm yourself," Mr. Ballin noted calmly, half smiling. "The lass is no worse for her looks." His blue eyes danced mischievously.

"It is Miss Strowne to you, sir."

"Ah, and see how calm she becomes," he quipped.

"If you had a care for your master you would not encourage . . ."

"No more," Audacia interrupted, throwing her gloves down upon the table.

The housekeeper tossed her head scornfully at the man who served as butler-valet-workman to Sir Aderly. Concern filled her again as she took in the disheveled, snow-covered figure before her. As her eyes went over the young woman they halted midway and widened in surprise. She stepped haltingly backward, fear spreading over her features.

"Now what is wrong, Miss Bea?" Audacia asked, taking a step closer.

"No, no. Stay where you are," the housekeeper begged, putting out a hand to stay the young woman. "Don't come any closer until you tell me what causes that." She pointed to one side of Audacia's greatcoat that was bobbing in and out.

The young woman looked down. "Oh, dear, I almost forgot." Reaching carefully inside, she smiled reassuringly at Miss Bea as she withdrew the furry mound. "It is only a tiny rabbit."

Letting out a long sigh of relief, the housekeeper relaxed, then straightened stiffly. "How can such a tiny thing have caused you to look as if you've been handled by some ruffian? And why are you covered with snow? Even the collar of your father's greatcoat is torn," she said assessing Audacia's state closely.

"I must have—have caught it on a branch, and I merely stumbled in the snow," she added brushing the snow from her breeches and the greatcoat. "Mr. Ballin, please take this and place it with the other creatures."

"Aye, miss, but what of your father? He was wantin' some lard to grease his machine."

"I'll see to that. See that you give the poor thing water and some feed," Audacia ordered as she shrugged out of the greatcoat.

"You best hurry," he told her as he left the kitchen.

Throwing the greatcoat across a chair, Audacia went to the cabinet and got out the crock of lard. "I'll see to mending the coat as soon as I've taken this to Father, Miss Bea. Could you brew me some tea? I feel chilled to the bones and it looks like more snow will be falling." With a grimace, she set the crock on the table. After retrieving the hair pins from her long black hair, she deftly twisted the heavy mane into a neat bun and pinned it in place. "There," she said to Miss Bea, "isn't that better?" Whistling, she took the heavy crock and left the kitchen to go toward her father's workshop, which had been attached to the east side of the house after their move there some four and ten years before.

A few tsks escaped the housekeeper as she set a kettle of water on the stove and then stirred the coal within. Now the girl whistles, she thought; how will she ever make a suitable match?

"Ballin, where have you been?" Sir Maurice Aderly scolded as the door closed behind Audacia.

"It is I, Father. Mr. Ballin is doing a task for me. Here is the lard." She set the crock on a nearby worktable. "How does the work progress?" she asked, sitting upon the table and swinging her legs to and fro as she viewed the assortment of rods, metal flanges, nuts, bolts, and other pieces her father was working with.

"Not well, not well at all. I do not think I shall use the lard after all." Her father's smooth brow wrinkled beneath receding wisps of hair.

"The adjustment you spoke of last eve at supper was a failure then?"

"No . . . yes." He straightened his large form and wiped his hands clean. "What have you been up to this morn?" His kind gray eyes took in Audacia's flushed cheeks and the breeches covering her legs. "Shall I be receiving another lecture from Miss Bea on your deportment?"

Audacia tossed her head to dismiss his question. "I had heard Squire Webster was allowing hunting . . ." she began her explanation.

"Now you object to a killer dog being bagged? Come, come, my girl," Sir Maurice scolded, picking up a wrench and turning to view his machine.

"I did not *know* it was a killer dog they were after. Why did you not speak of it if you had heard? Anyway, Geoffrey had promised to leave off hunting the poor creatures of the woods till summer."

"When you know hunting is no sport," laughed her father. He bobbed the wrench at her. "You cannot change the world, my dear. Englishmen have always been hunters."

"But you aren't, Father," she protested.

"Only because I chose not to," he clipped. Tinkering on

17

the machine, he told her, "I have hopes of perfecting this machine before this year's harvest begins. Think what it would mean to the farmers of England—to all of us. Why, if it is as efficient as the threshing machines, the production of grain can be doubled, tripled!" His face took on that dreamy look Audacia was all too familiar with.

"Yes, Father," she dutifully agreed, jumping lightly to her feet. "I am certain Mr. Ballin will return soon." Audacia waited for a moment, wishing to tell her father of the morning's incident in the woods, but Sir Aderly was no longer aware of her presence as he tightened a bolt here and adjusted a belt there upon his experimental harvester.

A glimmer of a frown passed through Audacia's eyes, now the brilliant blue of her flannel shirt. "I do hope it will go better for you this afternoon," she tossed to her father; then picking up a tune, she went humming from the workroom.

"I'll take the tea to my room," Audacia told Miss Bea, picking up the tray filled with the necessaries from the kitchen table. Seeing the disapproval upon the other, she added, "But you may bring me a light lunch. Some of the soup you made yesterday and a few slices of fresh bread, with butter, please. And"—she halted at the door—"some of that pigeon pie would be good. Was there any pudding left?"

"A 'light' lunch, miss?" Miss Bea asked with just a gleam of humor.

"Of course it is light. I'll have none of the brisket," laughed Audacia. "I can come and eat here if you wish."

"No, miss. It isn't fitting for the lady of the house to eat in the kitchen. I'll bring it up directly."

18

Concern flickered over Audacia's face. "You shouldn't be doing so much. Perhaps I should speak to Mary Correl about coming during the day to help."

"I see no need for that. There's only the four of us in this household and I haven't seen the day when I couldn't care for so few. It would be far more proper to see to the hiring of an abigail for you, miss," the housekeeper answered, taking advantage of the conversation to put forth her oft-espoused wish.

"And what would she do for me," Audacia asked laughingly as she eased the door open with her elbow, "undo my breeches?" After a wink at the shocked Miss Bea, she left.

"Poor Miss Bea," Audacia murmured aloud as she fastened the last button on her day frock. "It must be very trying for the good soul," she added while hanging the flannel shirt and breeches neatly in the armoire. She then took out a blue wool shawl and draped it across her shoulders to ward off the January chill, for the fire in her room was a small one and did little more than keep the chill from the vicinity of the fireplace.

Audacia's bedchamber was on the west end of the second floor of the red, Keuper sandstone house. Her father's bedchamber and two others, now unused, a sitting room, and a sewing room occupied the remainder of the floor. On the floor beneath was the morning room, oddly named since father and daughter supped there, and a large and a small parlor—the latter long ago taken over by her father's books and papers. Miss Bea's realm was the kitchen, scullery, and her own small room at the far end, while Mr. Ballin ruled the solarium, workroom, and his own

19

small chambers just off it. Not too far from the house, in view of Audacia's room, was the barn—a haven to Sir Aderly's elderly grays and their lone cow as well as to the young woman's numerous rescued animals.

Sir Aderly, his two children, and Miss Strowne had moved to the dull-rose red stone home near Bedworth shortly after the death of his wife. In his grief the baronet had sold his comfortable home in Grosvenor Square and purchased this modest farm of 500 acres, which had a comfortable (for his habits) yearly income of £500. Leasing the land out to neighboring farmers had proven highly satisfactory to Sir Aderly as it freed him entirely for his agricultural experiments and inventions. Only a small plot, used for experimenting with grains, was still under his control. The past four and ten years had given little variation to the Aderly children as their father lost himself in his workshop or bolted off to meetings with Watt, Wilkinson, and other experimenters in Edinburgh and London.

The biggest alteration in their lives had been four years hence when Daniel, at age four and ten, had been sent off to school. This, however, had been far too late to prevent Audacia from having aped and adopted all her younger brother's ways. Hard as the poor housekeeper had tried, the girl had grown up practicing few of the feminine niceties or habits deemed essential by society, especially the London "ton." Preferring the tomboyish ways she was long accustomed to, Audacia used the city-bred manners Miss Bea drilled into her only as she chose. The housekeeper, though doubtful of success, had never given up the prospect of awakening Sir Aderly to the need for refinement in his daughter's ways. Thus far she had never quite managed to separate him from his machinery experiments long enough to be successful, and her love for the young miss came through even the worst of her scolds, rendering them fruitless and assuring Audacia that there was little need for what Miss Bea called the "essentials of genteel behavior."

The common folk about Bedworth had accepted the warm, loving, motherless girl from her arrival in their midst, and had long laughed at her boyish mannerisms. The local gentry, however, especially the leading women, had taught Audacia as she reached the stage of young womanhood to use discretion by their disapproval and sometimes by overtly excluding her from social events. The gossip that Miss Aderly went about in breeches at times provoked expressions of disapproval, but nothing was done as no one had seen her in such attire or at least they were not telling if they had. For the past few years Audacia had made an uneasy truce with the more snobbish leaders of the local gentry, and her "peculiarities" were overlooked, if not overdiscussed, because of her motherless upbringing and the neglect of an eccentric father. Since she showed no signs of having designs on any of their sons, they were content to let her take part in social functions in the spirit of "charity."

The sons of the gentry, on the other hand, accepted Audacia with an easy camaraderie; the daughters with an envious friendship. At one time or another one and all came to her for advice. It seemed that human and animal alike sensed her empathy and sought sympathy, encouragement, or the friendly understanding of her silence.

Audacia's life had been monitored to a degree by the fact that she had spent long hours helping her father. The arrival of Mr. Ballin two years before had freed her from this, and she had taken to wandering the countryside as well as refereeing Mr. Ballin's and Miss Bea's constant antagonistic behavior towards each other.

All of the young women Audacia's age had long since been given a coming-out ball and had gone to London for the "season" each year since their sixteenth birthdays. If she was troubled by her lack in this area or by the fact that most were becoming engaged or were already wed, it was never evident in her behavior. Of late, however, she had found herself restless, but blamed this upon the confinement caused by the unusually snowy winter.

In her room Audacia poured her tea while she sat in the rocker before the two large windows that overlooked the woods behind the house. Outdoors, a battle among the blue tits, feeding on crumbs and grain the housekeeper had strewn about for them on the snow, caught her attention. She watched as a smaller bird huddled over a scrap of bread despite a great tit's complaints. Suddenly the thought came to Audacia that Geoffrey's friend was like the great tit. Strong, surely brave, but refusing to use his full strength against one who was weaker. Setting her teacup down, she wrapped the shawl more closely about her as a chill followed the remembrance of the look in the man's eyes when he had removed his hand. An uneasy feeling hovered close. Those dark eyes, she thought, they held . . . pain . . . torment.

"How could that be?" she spoke softly aloud. "You gazed in them for only a moment." But instinctively certain she was right, Audacia frowned, wondering why the thought distressed her.

CHAPTER III

Like a soft cloak thrown over the land, the late February snowfall concealed much that an earlier melting had revealed. The hungry water hen plodded slowly along the side of the river, her search for food a dismal failure. Catching sight of a flicker of movement, of a tiny splash of color, on the opposite bank, she gave a soft quack. The twisting bob of her head betrayed her hope that it was some beetle digging its way to the surface. A hasty check assured the hen that the surface of the river was covered with snow, a sign that it was solidly frozen. With quick swinging steps she began her dash to the other side. Midway across her weight broke the knife-thin crust of ice and snow and she found herself floundering in the ice-laced water. Quacking in loud, terrified honks, she kicked at the ice edge, trying to climb back onto the surface, only to have it crumble beneath her clawed feet.

The clamor drew the attention of two figures. The one

on foot was closer and also surer of the direction and thus reached the scene first.

Audacia, her father's old greatcoat now repaired and bundled tightly about her, with her brother's breeches and boots showing beneath it, quickly assessed the situation as she took in the water hen's plight. Left alone, the bird would surely freeze to death as the ice closed about it; she had no choice but to rescue it.

Casting about, she saw a forked branch in a dead tree, which she easily broke away. Audacia then carefully began edging her way toward the still struggling hen. Crooning softly, she tried to calm the bird so that she could use the branch as a fork and simply lift the trapped animal out of the water and back onto the ice. With each movement forward Audacia listened intently for the telltale cracking sound which would signal the thinning of the ice. She held her breath as she came within the branch's reach of the hen and slowly bent forward, trying to maneuver its crotch beneath the bird. Then she heaved slowly and steadily. Up went the branch carrying the bird haphazardly along with it. The panicked flapping of the hen's wings carried it from the branch and it landed a short distance from the hole in the ice on a thickness able to carry its weight.

Just as Audacia sighed with relief at the bird's safety, a loud snap cracked in the cold air and she felt her feet sink through the breaking ice.

Arriving at the scene in time to see the greatcoat-clad figure heave the hen to freedom, and then sink into the water, a horseman jumped from his mount at the river's edge. "Try to stay afloat, lad," he yelled as he strove to break a sturdy branch from the same dead tree. Finding it resisted his efforts, he climbed above it and soon severed it with a few well-placed kicks. The man carried it halfway to where the purple-hatted figure struggled to get a hold on the ice.

"The lad from yester month," Lord Greydon said aloud in surprise. He stretched full length upon the ice and pushed the branch forward toward the bobbing figure.

"Take the greatcoat off. Unfasten it," Greydon urged, seeing that the weight of the wet garment was pulling the figure beneath the water.

Her teeth chattering like castanets and her fingers so numb they were like blocks of wood, Audacia strove to undo the coat and stay afloat. At last it sank from her arms to the bottom of the river, but her strength had nearly been spent by the effort.

"Grab hold of the branch. Take hold. Try!" Lord Greydon urged. "The branch, lad, take hold!"

Audacia reached out, but it seemed her body was responding in slow motion. Desperation gripped her as the branch seemed to draw away when she forced her hand towards it. After a seeming eternity that lasted only seconds she managed to wrap first one hand, then the other around the stout branch Greydon was holding out to her across the ice.

His lordship pulled on the branch and though the ice at first broke under Audacia's weight, it finally held within arm's distance of him. Grabbing the wrist of the frigid victim, he pulled her free and dragged her to the river's edge.

Audacia's skin was tinged with blue as she lay upon the snow-covered ground; the white cover was melted by the water dripping from her soaked clothing. In one smooth

25

motion, Greydon removed his many-caped coat and wrapped it about the shivering figure. "Is there a cottage, any building, near here?" he asked as he fastened the large coat about the prone figure.

Nodding her head, she managed, "To—to—the—east," between chattering teeth. A violent tremor shook her. "Watch—for—for—the—"

"The smoke," Greydon finished for her. With easy movements he swept the thoroughly chilled figure into his arms and approached his mount. "Could you manage to stay in the saddle?" he asked looking down at the pale, bluish face.

Closed eyes and faint breath gave answer to his question.

"Now what, my man?" Greydon asked himself as he looked from the unconscious figure in his arms to his mount. Thinking back to his army days in Portugal and on the Continent, he shifted the "boy" to one arm as if he were a sack of cabbages. Holding his burden thus, he stepped into the saddle. With the bundle laid facedown across the saddle's edge before him, Greydon urged his steed to the east.

A short distance ahead he spied a trail of smoke in the sky. Kicking his mount to a faster run, he reached the gamekeeper's small cottage in moments. A quick vault backward from his mount landed him on his feet, and stepping to the horse's side he snatched the "lad's" form from the saddle. Hard kicks upon the cottage's door announced his presence.

Upon opening the door, the startled gamekeeper's wife gaped at the tall gentleman as he strode past her to the fireplace without invitation. A boy of nine came from one

26

corner of the cottage and peered over Greydon's shoulder as he unfastened the coat from the figure he laid before the fire.

"Get me blankets," his lordship snapped at Mrs. Stollard, who was still standing at the door. "Can't you see this lad is soaked to the skin and near frozen. It'll be his death if we don't get him dried and warmed."

"But we've only those on our bed," she protested.

"Get them." Returning his attention to the unconscious figure, Lord Greydon untied the bindings of the purple cap from beneath the softly rounded chin and was surprised to find a mass of coal-black hair beneath it when he pulled it off.

"Pull the boots off," he ordered the young boy as he grabbed hold of the wet flannel shirt to tear it off. There was a sound of rending cloth and then his lordship's eyes widened as his gaze rested upon a woman's bodice. An odd flicker passed over his face. "By all the bloody . . ."

Mrs. Stollard returned to his side at this instant with the blankets. Looking down, she drew her breath in sharply.

"What's the matte', mum?" the young lad asked.

"Nothin', Ned," she answered draping the blankets quickly across the prone figure. "Ye fetch yerself over to Sir Aderly's. Tell his man to bring their carriage right away."

"They won't be believin' me, mum," he protested.

"Ye tell them I said an accident has happened and they should hurry," she insisted.

"But they've no boy stayin' with them."

"If you don't want yer backside warmed ye'll see to it," his mother snapped angrily.

"Do you know where this Aderly lives?" Greydon asked the boy.

"Aye, milord, I do," Ned answered, cocking his head questioningly.

"Get your coat on and do as your mother has told you. Here." His lordship put a half crown in the lad's hand. "Hurry now."

"I'll run all the way, milord," the boy answered excitedly.

"Tell them to bring warm wrappings and some warming pans," Mrs. Stollard threw in as the lad grabbed his ragged coat from the wall.

"Aye, mum," the boy answered, already shrugging into his coat. Halting at the door he looked to the finely dressed gentleman.

"Run as fast as you can."

With a nod he bolted out of the door and down the lane leading from the cottage.

"Let me help get those wet clothes off her," Greydon told the gamekeeper's wife, going down on one knee at Audacia's side.

"Would you have her freeze to death?" he responded to the woman's steely-eyed stare and moved to the young woman's feet. He removed the boots from one foot, then the other.

"I don't know how Miss Audacia got in the hands o' the likes o' ye," Mrs. Stollard said as she tugged the clinging wet flannel from Audacia's arms, "but ye can put aside yer notions, no matter what they be."

"Unfasten those buttons," he commanded her, ignoring what she had said and pointing to the breeches.

"Milord, I . . ." the startled woman took exception.

28

"Your attitude is understandable but absolutely absurd, I assure you," he told her, reaching himself to undo the buttons.

A sharp slap to his hand made him withdraw it. Huffily Mrs. Stollard undid the breeches' fastenings.

"Thank you," Greydon quipped and pulled one of the blankets over the wet breeches. "If you take hold of this, and I the breeches, we can remove them without damage to this lady's 'sensibilities,' " he noted sarcastically.

His lordship soon learned it required more than a gentle tug to divest the prone figure of her wet, clinging, lower covering. "This young miss needs to be advised to stay away from the pantry or make suitable adjustments in her garments," he noted exasperatedly.

"Milord, they are wet," clucked Mrs. Stollard, her eyes telling him how indelicate a subject he had broached.

"Do you have a nightdress we . . . I mean you,"—he altered his choice of words to forestall the scold—"can put on her?"

"If ye'll be steppin' outside I do," she returned, rubbing Audacia's hands. "The poor thing is near froze."

"Enough of this squabbling," Greydon snorted walking around to Audacia's head. "Fetch the nightdress. Two can get it on her much faster than one and stop your scowling. I've seen women before."

"Fancy that," the older woman scoffed. "A braggart no less," she snorted angrily, refusing to let go of the blanket that covered Audacia.

"I didn't mean this particular one," he returned with infuriated seriousness. "What use have I for a breech-sporting twig. I prefer my ladies to be . . . women."

Audacia stirred and moaned.

"Your defense of her honor is noted but she'll have no use for it if she does not live." He pulled a silver flask from his jacket. Opening it, he set it to Audacia's lips and poured some of the dark liquid within into her mouth, then pinched her nose shut, forcing her to swallow.

Mrs. Stollard, having yielded to the truth of his argument, had gotten her nightdress, a heavy coarse linen billow of cloth, but paused as she returned to the young woman's side.

"Would it be more suitable if I closed my eyes?" his lordship offered, irritated by the woman's hesitancy.

"Aye, milord, and see that there's no peekin'," she answered with relief at the solution to her quandary.

Closing his eyes, Greydon lifted Audacia's shoulders from the hearth's surface. Between them they managed to get her into the gown. Then the earl again gave Audacia a dose of spirits and was rewarded by coughing and fluttering eyelids. "Rub her feet—get some color back into them," he commanded the gamekeeper's wife. Putting his arm beneath Audacia's shoulders as she coughed again, he leaned her against him. Her wet hair soaked through his jacket and shirt immediately. With a curse he grabbed a coarse towel that was within arm's reach and began rubbing her head vigorously.

"I'm not . . . to . . . be . . . shaken . . . to death," came a weak protest from the victim of his ministrations.

"I should have known no thanks would be coming from you," the earl scoffed but eased the roughness of his motion.

With a shaking hand, Audacia raised the corner of the towel that continued to hang in her eyes. "Mrs. Stollard!

30

How did I come to be here?" she asked through clacking teeth.

"Ye ought ta be askin' the gentleman that, Miss Audacia. 'Tis he who brought ye here."

Tilting her head back, Audacia's eyes, now pale gray in her unusually pallid face, encountered the dark, half-concerned, half-angry eyes of Lord Greydon. For a long moment an invisible bond held them. Then recognition came. "You—y-you," she stuttered, her words and actions still slowed by the numbness of her body. "Leave . . . go . . . of . . . me," she demanded haltingly.

Instantly he rose and she fell back against the hearth with a dull thud.

"Why . . . you . . . oaf," she said, wrenching herself to a sitting position and drawing the blankets about her and edging closer to the fire.

"The next time I find you drowning in mid-winter, please remind me only to bid you the time of day as I pass by," Greydon told her with a slight bow.

"Oh, you . . ."

"I do think the lady will recover," he told Mrs. Stollard. "Since I am no longer needed I shall take my leave," Greydon said, bowing gracefully to the gamekeeper's wife.

"Ye don't mean it milord," she protested. "Sir Aderly, what be I ta tell him? He'll be certain ta want ta speak with ye."

"Tell him nothing. I am a stranger here and little likely to meet him. His 'lad' came to no harm with me." The earl turned to Audacia. "I beg pardon 'miss,' for my rough treatment of you on our previous encounter and also hope the saddle bow was not too unpleasant . . . uncomfortable on our ride here but, then, I did not realize that you were a 'lad' of such delicate persuasions." His tone altered as he swung back to Mrs. Stollard. "Have her finish what is in the flask."

"I'll take nothing of yours," Audacia retorted, angered by his superior manner and the fact that she could neither halt the clattering of her teeth nor the shivering tremors running through her limbs.

"But I insist," he bowed and half smiled at the attempted wrathful look his action drew from the young woman, for it merely brought out for the first time to his sight the womanly lines of her features. His exit was hasty as he saw Audacia grab for the flask and raise her arm.

The thud of it against the door sounded behind his back. "Fine thanks," he muttered. "A cold ride this shall be," he continued, talking aloud to himself as he mounted. Greydon took one last look at the cottage. "A sickening chill wouldn't dare lay hold of that wench," he assured himself. Her parents will be coming soon, his rationalizing spirit added. If I don't want to be held accountable for compromising the creature, I had best be gone, he thought.

As he kicked his mount to a run, a pair of pale gray eyes appeared in his mind's eye—one moment full of innocence, the next full of as much spirit as he'd ever seen.

CHAPTER IV

"Are you bloody well gone daft," Squire Webster greeted his slightly frozen friend. "Riding on a day like this without proper clothing. "What is that?" he pointed to the darkened area of Greydon's jacket. "Why it is wet—frozen stiff. You'll take a death of a chill for certain. Whatever have you been doing?"

"Stop clucking like a nanny," Greydon threw at him, his usual concern for his friend's feelings put aside. "You're a fine one to carry on when it is your fault. Is there a fire in the library?" he asked, reaching the stairs on which Geoffrey stood.

"Yes. You don't mean to go there," the squire added when Greydon turned and began walking in that direction. "Surely you shall change first."

"If my attire displeases you, you—no. Come with me, Geoff. There are a few answers I would have from you."

"Answers? Have you emptied that flask you always

carry with you? Let me see it." Geoffrey followed his unanswering friend, concern mounting.

In the library Greydon poured a liberal dose of port from the decanter on a side table and carried the glass to the fireplace. Quaffing a good half of it, he set the glass on the mantel and held his hands out to the fire to warm them.

"Are you going to tell me what you have been about?" Webster asked, joining him.

"I was just about to ask you the same," the other noted with the whisp of sarcasm usually directed at himself. He took hold of his glass and finished the port. Coughing as the dark liquid raced down his throat, he recovered then sneezed and felt a shivering tremor run through his body as he realized how cold he was.

"There, you have taken a chill." Geoffrey pulled the bellcord and the butler came immediately. "Have coal added to the fire in his lordship's chamber and have the bed warmed. Tell his man to lay out night clothing," he ordered and turned back to his friend. "Now, Roland, off to your bedchamber."

"First I shall have some answers. That 'lad' we encountered, so to speak, last month. Did you know who 'he' was?"

"The lad? What lad?" Webster asked with contrived seriousness.

"Doing it a bit too brown for my tastes, Geoff, seeing as that situation gave you such good humor. *Achoo!*" Greydon ended with a violent sneeze.

"You had a perfectly good—no, I must say, stylish— caped coat when you arrived here, my friend. Why would you not wear it on such a cold day?" Geoffrey remarked, hoping to change the course of the conversation.

"That will not do. *Achoo* . . . Geoff, I will have my answer."

"Not until you are abed," the squire amended, starting to walk toward the doors. "When you have gotten yourself to bed I will answer all of your questions about the 'lad.' It wouldn't be that he is the cause of this chill, would it?" Geoffrey asked with a raised eyebrow and hurried his steps from the room at the thunderous expression upon his friend's face.

"Miss Strowne! Miss Strowne, open the door, quickly now," called Sir Aderly as he and Mr. Ballin struggled up the flagstone walk to the front door with their awkward burden.

"Father, put me down this instant," Audacia's muffled voice commanded angrily, her spirit of sportliness nonexistent after being rolled in a woolen blanket and carried like a carpet taken out to be dusted. "I told you I can walk. Now put me down."

"Remember your manners, miss," Sir Maurice snapped, his usual humor gone under the strain of finding that his only daughter had nearly drowned and that her reputation may have been compromised by a stranger. With the door properly closed behind then, Sir Aderly let go of his end of the wriggling bundle, dropping Audacia ungently to the oak floor.

"Sir Aderly . . . what is this?" Miss Strowne asked, taken aback by his look and manner. "Is that Miss Audacia's voice I hear inside that—But the lad said someone had almost drowned?" She looked to Sir Maurice, who nodded at the unspoken question. "Oh, Lord, is she safe?"

"In as fine a voice as the lass has ever been," Mr. Ballin threw out with a broad smile upon his face as he untied the rope about his end of the blanket.

"Whatever were you thinking of, wrapping her like a cod," Miss Strowne scolded, reaching down to untie the other end as the young woman within kicked wildly.

"Ah, I knew you had it in you, if ever you'd find it," Ballin quipped with a wink at Miss Bea. "Ain't humor grand?"

"Father," Audacia spluttered, preventing the housekeeper from venting words upon the butler. "What is the reason for this treatment?" she ended, her head freed at last. "Surely you don't believe the ramblings of Mrs. Stollard? She is far afield with her wild thoughts."

"You are to get yourself to your chamber immediately, young woman," Sir Maurice roared, "and garb yourself in clothes befitting your sex. Mrs. Stollard is absolutely correct in her assumptions. If it had not been for her quick-wittedness, her lad, Ned, would have seen it was you the man rescued and the entire countryside would be agaggle with the gossip."

"But, Father," she began to protest.

"To your chamber," he commanded, his deep tone and outstretched, pointing arm brooking no rebuttal.

Angrily kicking her feet free from the blanket, Audacia rose haughtily, insult plainly written across her features. Wrapped in the many-caped cloak with the dangling sleeves that concealed her hands she struck a comical pose.

At the sight the harshness eased in Sir Aderly's face. "I

shall speak with you later on this and at some length," he told her as she turned to go.

Audacia tossed her head but her bottom lip trembled. A look towards Miss Bea, who stood wondering what ghastly thing had occurred, and then one toward Mr. Ballin, who stood with his hands clasped behind his back, his bowed head unsuccessfully concealing a broad grin, was all that was needed to send her running up the stairs toward her chamber, ready to burst into tears.

"Sir Aderly, what has happened?" Miss Strowne asked as she watched the retreating figure out of sight.

Nodding to her to wait, Aderly gruffly instructed, "Mr. Ballin, see to the team and carriage and then come to the workshop."

"Aye, sir, in the bloomin' of a flower's time," Ballin answered, winking wickedly at the housekeeper.

"Now, Miss Strowne, would you please come to the parlor with me?" Sir Maurice asked, running his finger around his neck to loosen his cravat.

"Of course, Sir Aderly," Miss Bea replied, completely mystified by this turn. She followed him into the parlor and sat as he motioned her to do. Arranging the folds of her full gray skirt, she awaited his words.

Sir Aderly, however, began striding nervously back and forth before her. "Miss Bea, it is not my habit to discuss matters concerning the family with servants."

"Assuredly," she murmured.

"But one could say that you are in a sense a family member, having been with us from the beginning of my marriage," he continued. "Lady Aderly respected your judgment on all matters."

"Why, thank you, sir." The housekeeper straightened proudly.

"Ahem," Sir Aderly cleared his throat and halted before her, giving her a stern look. Slowly, his large frame slumped; a bewildered look came over him. "A man is not fit to raise a daughter alone," he sighed and sat heavily in a chair across from Miss Strowne. "You must realize"—his eyes met hers—"that you have warned me this could happen. Not this but something similar."

"I, sir? But . . . ?"

"Hear my words before you speak. When I have finished what I must say, then I will listen to your thoughts," Sir Maurice instructed her. "What transpired today, hopefully, will have no ill effects, but it has given me ample proof of the truth of your words.

"Fortunately, Mrs. Stollard, the gamekeeper's wife, was wise enough to keep her lad from recognizing Audacia and wrapped her as she was; no one could see who it was that we brought home with us. Mr. Ballin suggested we tell those who asked that a nephew of his was visiting and went out alone. But we'll think on that later. Now, all Ned knows is that a lad was rescued from the river by a gentleman, a stranger who must be visiting someone in the area. From the look of the coat she wore . . . yes, it must have belonged to the stranger." Sir Aderly answered Miss Bea's gasp at mention of the coat. "Under ordinary conditions I would have Ballin out scouring the countryside to learn my daughter's rescuer's name but circumstances prevent that."

"Oh, my," breathed Miss Bea, her alarm growing.

"Yes, I cannot even thank the man who saved my daughter's life for fear the consequences of it becoming common knowledge would prove worse than her drowning. He bloody well had better be an honorable man," Aderly added as if saying a prayer. Continuing after a brief pause, he told the housekeeper, "Evidently the man pulled Audacia from the river not far from the gamekeeper's cottage, on Squire Webster's land. Mrs. Stollard said that he thought my daughter was a lad, until he undid her shirt."

"Oh, my, no!" exclaimed Miss Bea, aghast.

"I am sorry to be this indelicate, Miss Strowne, and I must add that Mrs. Stollard stepped in at that point and nothing untoward occurred. But you can imagine what will happen if word of this reaches the local gentry. Those fal-lal, snippity women will take hold of it with a passion. Audacia will be shunned," he ended coldly. Sir Aderly rubbed his eyes. "If only she had not been in those confounded breeches!" Rising agitatedly, he spoke harshly, "You warned me, but I could not see the harm."

"But surely this man will not speak to others of this? Surely he will know the effect it would have on Miss Audacia if he does? Perhaps he does not know who she is and will think it matters not?" Miss Bea offered hopefully.

"Much will depend on the kind of man he is. So many of the London dandies I have been acquaintenced with would banter such a happening at every chance, to anyone willing to listen. We can but pray he is not one of these.

"Meanwhile, I must take action to lessen the damage if it proves the man is a babbler. It is your opinion on an idea that has come to me that I must now have."

"You know I would do anything for Miss Audacia, sir. Tell me what you would do," Miss Bea assured him.

"Do you recall Lady Darby?" Sir Maurice asked.

"Yes, but what has her ladyship to do with . . ." The housekeeper ended her words at the look of annoyance on the baronet's face and nodded.

"As you know, Lady Darby was a very close friend of my dear wife's and after Lady Aderly's death she told me that she would gladly take on the task of presenting Audacia to society. I am not up to the 'ton,' as I hear society is now referred to, but Lady Darby has always traveled in only the best circles. It is my thought to send Audacia, under the proper escort of an abigail, to her ladyship. She and her husband should be returning to London soon for the season—an event Lady Darby would never miss. Their country home is in Worcester, not too long a drive from here for this time of year.

"The journey would take Audacia away for a time and perhaps even result in a match for her. I believe the Darbys have a son near her age. I fear I have been very neglectful of my daughter." Sir Maurice shook his head sadly. "And I can only hope it is not too late to make amends." He looked hopefully at the housekeeper. "What do you think of the scheme? Speak the truth now."

An all-encompassing smile wreathed Miss Bea's face. "It is all I dreamed of for Miss Audacia," she responded. "The perfect answer. It suits very well, indeed, sir."

"Good to hear you agree, Miss Strowne, for I have decided you should be abigail to Audacia," Sir Maurice told her confidently and rose from his chair.

"Abigail!" squeaked Miss Bea. "But I am a housekeeper," she protested. "Oh, I know I was abigail to Lady Aderly before you married, sir, but really now, all I've done for years is tend to the needs of your home."

40

"And managed very well," Sir Aderly praised her. "And you shall be my housekeeper again when you and Audacia return home, never fear."

"But, Sir Aderly, I know nothing about being an abigail in this day. And what would happen to you and Mr. Ballin if I should go? Oh, no, sir—I cannot," she ended, rising in her turmoil.

"Miss Strowne, don't you see that it can be no one else? You know Audacia, her whims and all her behavior. Only you could handle her, keep her from innocent but harmful mischief," Sir Maurice attempted to persuade her.

Blanching, Miss Bea thought of the results of Miss Audacia being set loose upon London.

Pressing his advantage, Aderly continued. "Think of the result if I was to get an abigail of Audacia's own age, or even one more mature who did not realize her caprices. You, Miss Strowne, now you could be masterful with her. What has she not attempted with you? You are wise beyond your years when it comes to her ways," he said grinning sheepishly. "Perhaps I should have listened to you long ago. Come, will you not help me now?"

"I—I cannot think it suits, sir. Why, I cannot imagine you and Mr. Ballin on your own," she objected, but weakly.

"Ballin assures me he is handy with the pots, and surely you could arrange for one of the local girls to come in and straighten things, as it were."

Still Miss Bea nodded no.

"If you will not, there is no answer. Audacia must remain here. We can only hope for the best," Sir Aderly said with sad resignation.

"You—you think this man will boast of having seen . . . ?"

"Mrs. Stollard told me that even when the man realized that the lad he rescued was my daughter he still was very sharp and 'uppity,' to use her words. What greater on-dit could he have to please his host, or to share with his drinking chums at the nearest inn. The little knowledge I have of such gentry is not reassuring."

"Then . . . then I shall consent to your plan. But Miss Audacia? Have you told her of it?" the housekeeper asked with concern.

"I shall do that this eve after we sup. For the moment take her some strong tea, for she was soaked dreadfully in that cold river. I shall ready a letter for Ballin to post announcing your arrival to Lord and Lady Darby," Sir Aderly told her enthusiastically.

"But don't you think it wise to seek their opinion on when we should come?" Miss Bea asked cautiously.

"A woman's thinking, Miss Strowne. They will be pleased to help me in this matter. Audacia is not unpretty and *can* be well mannered. Off with you. Go see to her. I must write that letter." He waved dismissal.

"Oh," the baronet sighed aloud as he walked to the small parlor and sat at his desk. "So lucky to have come through this with so little damage done. Perhaps 'twill even prove a blessing in the end."

Then he thought of Audacia as she had looked sitting on his workshop table, her face aglow from her walk in the cold, her brother's breeches scandalously clothing her legs. Somehow this did not match the idea of a docile young miss coming into society, for to his eyes young misses had always looked like milky shadows who would not dare stray from their maternally plotted courses. Was he wrong to send Audacia into the midst of such? What chance would she have without the guidance of her mother?

CHAPTER V

"Is something amiss, Father?" Audacia asked at supper.
"Your appetite is poor indeed, not to do justice to one of
Miss Bea's roasts of lamb."

"There is nothing wrong with me, but I cannot understand how you can sit there and eat as if nothing occurred
this day. The excitement should have set you in high
whoops. Why most ladies would still be hysterical," noted
Sir Aderly. "At the least you should have a decent case of
the sniffles."

"You know I enjoy good health, Father. I was not wet
that long. The gentleman's more to be pitied for he had
to ride without his cloak."

"Did he happen to mention with whom he was visiting?" Sir Aderly asked, raising a cautious eye from his
plate.

"We were not on an outing, Father. I do not even know
his name, but I was thinking how cold he would be with

neither his cloak nor his flask to warm him," Audacia observed before taking another healthy bit of roast.

"Have you no gratitude, child? The man did save your life," her father returned gruffly.

Miss Bea peered cautiously into the morning room as she paused in the doorway, then came forward and set a bowl of steamed carrots on the table. She glanced from father to daughter before hurriedly departing.

"I do think this afternoon has proven too much for Miss Bea," Audacia noted contritely in a whisper. "Ever since you and Mr. Ballin carried me in, she has gone about as if expecting a cannon to be fired at any time."

Coloring slightly, Sir Maurice renewed his pursuit of an exceptionally reluctant piece of lamb.

Little conversation was exchanged during the remainder of the meal. Indeed, Audacia thought it odd for her father to be so silent, for their evening meals were more often than not continuous discussions of his work and ideas for improving upon it. As was her habit, she rose when Ballin served Sir Aderly his glass of port and daily pipeful of tobacco.

"Audacia, I would like you to stay with me for a time yet," Sir Aderly said breaking his silence.

"If you wish, Father," she answered retaking her seat. "Did your work go poorly today?"

"My work? No, that is not what I have in mind to speak to you about."

"If it is about wearing Daniel's breeches, I promise to be very careful in the future," Audacia rushed to assure him.

"You are never to go about in them again. It is indecent." Sir Aderly's voice rose angrily. Taking a sip of port, he forced himself to become calm once more.

"I am sorry for today . . . that you are so distressed," Audacia told him earnestly as she leaned forward, her arms upon the table. Her gray eyes, which seemed to have borrowed some of the green from her dress, pled for forgiveness.

"It is not just today that worries me," Sir Maurice said, shifting his bulk in the Queen Anne chair, "but your future, child. I have been wrong to keep you here with me all these years. You should have gone to a lady's finishing academy. At least to London long ago as did your friends."

"But I care not for such foolishness," Audacia told him honestly. "What can London give me that I do not have here?"

"A chance for a good match," her father came to the point.

"But I could have that here if it was what I wanted. I have no desire to wed and leave you, Father."

"That is unnatural. All young women wish for a husband and a family of their own. It is the way of things. I mean to take steps soon to give you that opportunity," Sir Aderly told his daughter, sensing the opening he had sought.

Suspicion flared over Audacia's face. "What do you mean to do? Are we all to remove to London?"

"No."

Relief came with an audible sigh.

"You and Miss Strowne are to go to London. To stay with old family friends, Lord and Lady Darby. You must recall her ladyship, she was your godmother and the dear-

46

est of your mother's friends." The lack of reaction from his daughter made Sir Aderly pause.

"Do you mean the giggle-ridden lady whose son broke my spinning top?" Audacia asked with studied seriousness.

"How am I to recall that? How can you for a certainty? But, yes, Lady Darby was prone to . . . to gaiety in those years. You do remember her correctly. She will be most pleased to see you again," he rushed on.

"I will write her shortly then, if that is what you desire . . ."

"There is not need for you to correspond with her. Ballin has already posted my letter telling her ladyship that you and your abigail, Miss Strowne of course, shall be arriving by mail coach within the week."

"Within the week!" Audacia was now standing. "You cannot mean this, Father. Why, I cannot go. Who would care for my animals and . . . ?"

"You have no choice in this Audacia. I have not required much of you in the past. Now I ask this of you, that you go to Lady Darby and follow her guidance for the duration of the season. When it is at an end and Lady Darby removes once more to her Worcester home, you may return here." He rose, walked to his daughter's side, and took her hand in his. "Audacia, you are a young woman your mother would have been very proud of. She would want this. It is after all, only one spring in your life."

His gentle tone and loving gaze rocked Audacia's resistance. She wanted to shout "One spring—why must I give up any?" but she held back her words. Her father had asked little indeed and even this, she knew, was not asked for his benefit. Blinking back a tear, she managed, "Only if Mr. Ballin will care for the animals."

The windows of Lord Greydon's chambers on the upper floor of Web Manor twinkled warmly in the cold night air. Inside a fire burned brightly and candles cast their shadows across the large man reclining against the pillows propped behind him in the large canopied bed.

"I shall sit with his lordship," Squire Webster whispered to the valet who had risen at his entrance. As the man left, Geoffrey settled himself in an overstuffed high-backed chair situated before the fire so he could watch Greydon. Sipping at the port he had brought with him, he kept an attentive eye on his friend. His thoughts went to their time together in Spain and Portugal. Geoffrey gave himself a shake as he found his eyes had strayed to where his left arm should have rested on the chair's arm.

"Is it late, Geoff?" Greydon asked in a voice distorted by the chill he had taken.

"Not very . . . for you. But you have managed to sleep the afternoon and early evening away. How do you feel?" Webster asked, leaning forward in his chair.

"I don't think I really want to consider that. Find me a glass of brandy," Greydon grunted irritably.

"Oh, ho, my lord is out of sorts," Geoffrey quipped as he rose, poured a glass of brandy from the decanter in the chamber, and took it to his friend. As he returned to the table to pick up his own glass he jested lowly, "See, I am still useful."

Greydon inwardly winced at the words, a pain far different from the misery of his chill clouding his eyes. A tremor ran through him and he fretfully pulled the bedcovers closer about him. "Could the fire be built up? I am as cold as the ices I fetch for the ladies in the heat of July."

The squire set his glass upon the bedside table and pulled another comforter from the bottom of the bed to cover his friend. "I find it difficult to believe a man such as yourself would succumb so easily to a chill. You have not been taking proper care of yourself of late, I fear. I did not think you looked very rested when you first arrived and yet it has been well over four months since you sold out of the army."

Greydon's slightly feverish eyes avoided the squire's.

"We have been true friends, Roland. I owe you much . . . my life. Mayhaps we should talk of . . . of that time. I want you to know. I no longer resent your interference with my death."

"I wish you wouldn't, Geoff. I never held your words against you. Other men have said worse. Your looks, your actions—your enthusiasm for the future bloody well tell of your complete recovery. I marvel that you . . . have done so well." Lord Roland hurriedly drained his glass. "Fill this?" he asked, holding it out.

"Only one time more," Webster told him. "It would be better if you would eat. I could send for some broth."

"No, I feel no hunger." Greydon shook his head. He studied the back of his one-armed friend, the empty sleeve pinned up near the shoulder. "How did you do it, Geoff? How did you manage to forget it all?"

Was it the distortion of his voice or was it anguish he heard, Geoffrey asked himself as he walked slowly back to his friend's bedside, brandy in hand. "I haven't forgotten it, Roland. I've too constant a reminder for that. But I've put it behind me, slowly, surely, and with help."

49

"Help? Then someone has replaced Lucille in your affections?"

A shadow passed over Webster's face before he turned away. "Does she ever ask of me?" he asked in a strained voice.

"No, but sisters are an odd sort. She has never said a word. What happened, Geoff? Why weren't you two wed after you came home from Portugal? I had thought to come home an uncle."

"That is a cruel jest, Roland. I had thought better of you," Geoffrey clipped out, then waved his hand. "Let us say no more about it. You are not well and should rest."

"Pardon this damnable bore, Geoff. I've made a bloody mess of too many things of late. It would displease me greatly to lose your friendship," Greydon entreated in a quiet voice. "Remain awhile." He forced a more cheerful tone, saying, "You never did answer my question about the 'lad' and here I am"—he shifted into a sitting position on the pillows—"abed as you bid."

Geoffrey sat in the chair before the fireplace. A low chuckle escaped him. "I take it you have discovered the 'lad's' secret." His head was poised questioningly.

"Why did you not tell me at the time," Greydon grumbled. "I am not fond of making a bloody fool of myself."

"I thought you accounted very well for yourself," the squire said, raising his glass in salute. "Few come out of a scrap with Audacia as well as you managed."

"Now who is in high whoops," Lord Roland noted uncomfortably. "You know I would never have laid hands on her if I had but known."

"Let this thought ease your mind. Even had Audacia known that you are an earl of the realm she would not have been forestalled one wit. She has the greatest disregard for the proprieties of anyone I know."

"Just who is this Sir . . . Aderly? I believe that is what the woman at the cottage said the name was? Why does he allow his daughter to go about disguised? Even I am taken aback by her . . ." He stumbled for want of a word.

"Audacity?" the squire offered.

"Well, the chit is well named for all that." Greydon's features relaxed; a tenderness not there before came over him. "You know she has the most changeable eyes. They seem to take on whatever color she wears," he noted.

"Now I know why you were always chosen for reconnaissance duty, such keen observation, old friend." Webster's words were spoken earnestly enough, but the wide grin on his face betrayed his meaning. He ducked the pillow that Greydon hurled at him. "Should we think it is the chill that has disturbed your usually excellent aim, my lord, or has your heart—no, I surrender," he offered with a laugh as Greydon made to throw a second pillow. "As to who Sir Aderly is—he is a baronet. A widower with a son, Daniel, now at Oxford, and a daughter whom you have met, Audacia. They live in that smallish two-storey house we rode past about four days ago on one of our jaunts."

"The one where all the clattering and clanging was disturbing the countryside?"

"That was Sir Aderly at work. He is trying to perfect a harvesting machine . . . among other projects. He also tries to produce seed grains more suitable to our weather here. Quite a pleasant chap, really."

"It is surprising I never noticed Miss Aderly among the milksop squad of green girls loosed upon London this fall.

51

I cannot help but think she would stand out in such a group."

"Of a certainty. But Audacia has never been to London. At least not since Sir Aderly removed the family here. That was some five and ten years past, I believe. His wife had passed away and he sought to . . . to leave memories behind. I can understand that." Geoffrey looked away, attempting to conceal painful recollections.

"He never remarried?" Greydon asked, his empathy urging him to draw his friend from his sudden melancholy.

"No. A spinster housekeeper came with them and he seems perfectly content. But why all these questions about so unworthy a miss?" The squire's mood lightened. "Do I detect a note of interest?" Webster teased lightly.

"Ha! I have no need for a masquerading 'lad' to amuse me. Come to London and I shall show you women."

"Of that I have no doubts," Geoffrey said as he laughed in return. "And now that I have answered your questions you must tell me what occurred to deprive you of both your caped coat and your flask."

"It was nothing. I merely came across the 'lad' floundering in the river. Can you imagine anyone daft enough to risk thin ice for a water hen? I came to the river just in time to see this Miss Aderly heave the bird from the water, with a branch mind you, only to sink through the ice herself. After I managed to pull her free, she directed me to a nearby cottage. It was when I sought to divest the 'lad' of the wet garments that I discovered the reason for your good humor. Quite a jolt it was."

"I can well imagine Audacia's reaction. But how did you manage to get that far?"

"The girl was not in her senses," Lord Roland explained. "Fainted from the cold. The woman in the hut recognized her and immediately sent her boy, Ned . . ."

"Oh, the Stollards—but go on," the squire urged, eager to get all the facts.

"She sends this Ned to fetch Aderly and gives me a scold like I haven't had since I left my nanny's care. You'd think I compromised the girl," Greydon ended, his ire beginning to rise. "The chit herself was as thankless as the water hen when she came to her senses. Almost regret I pulled her from the river," he ended and finished his brandy.

Humor had left Webster. "If word of this gets abroad you *will* have compromised her. Did you speak to anyone? What did Sir Aderly have to say?"

"I wouldn't know. Left as soon as I was certain she was all right. Gave her my flask and coat. Wasn't that enough?" Greydon asked irritably. "What's your concern in this?"

"Audacia is . . . a . . . a dear friend. I won't have her harmed in any way. No one knows she goes about in her brother's clothing. Well, very few," he added at Greydon's skeptical look. "The local 'good' women will have her ostracized if they hear of this. Something must be done," Webster said agitatedly.

"Well, I won't marry the chit if that's what you have in mind," his lordship snorted and sneezed. "More than likely she hasn't even taken a chill." He sneezed again.

"I hope you are right about that and I doubt your liberty will need be surrendered," Geoffrey replied.

"Audacia has some rather set ideas on that subject. Sleep now. In the morn I shall ride over to Aderly's and see the lay of things. But"—Webster paused at the door—"you could choose a worse wife."

CHAPTER VI

"Good morn, Mr. Ballin," Squire Webster greeted the smiling butler. "I was hoping to speak with Miss Audacia, is she in?"

"A good day ta ye, Squire. I think Miss Audacia is in the barn with her animals. If ye wish I shall tell her ye have come," Ballin said with a bow.

"No, I'll just go there. I know the way. You needn't bother."

Ballin closed the door as the squire hurried through the crusted snow towards the barn.

"Who was that?" Miss Bea called, stopping at the foot of the stairs, her arms full of bed linens.

"Squire Webster callin' on Miss Audacia," he answered with a spritely wink.

"You had the good sense to tell him she was out, didn't you?" she asked refusing to be baited.

"Of course not. I directed him to the barn. Have ye no

romantic bones hidden within, Miss Bea?" Ballin asked, coming to her side and taking the bed linens.

"Miss Strowne to you, Mr. Ballin. And I can manage those myself," she said attempting to retrieve the sheets and pillowcases.

" 'Twould be most ungracious of me now," he replied. Starting up the stairs, he asked, "Wouldn't ye like ta see the squire and Miss Audacia make a match of it?"

"Why he's a cripple. It's a whole man I'll have for my miss," the housekeeper snapped.

"Ah, there's where ye be wrong, Miss Bea. There's far more a man could be lackin' than an arm. Me thinks he manages right well."

"The squire's a fine man. It's just that . . ."

"I know, Miss Bea," Ballin said, tossing a sad look over his shoulder. "There are many who think as ye do, for all yer good-heartedness. But think of this: Boney made many to be like the squire before he was put away for good. What are they to be doin' with their lives? Squire Webster's still a man, and better than most I've seen."

Ashamed of her words, Miss Bea grimaced uncomfortably as Ballin halted before the linen closet. "I—I meant nothing," she said under his accusing stare.

"I know, Miss Strowne," the short butler replied gently, "but it's those who speak unthinkin' like that can give the most hurt." He said no more as she took the different stacks, one at a time, and laid them in their proper places.

With regret for her words still visible on her face, Miss Bea heard Ballin say as she closed the door, "But I know ye didna' mean it, about the squire I mean." As she turned to him she broke into a weak smile at his sudden awkwardness.

"Why, Miss Bea, there's hope to be had still. 'Tis the first time ye actually smiled upon me," Ballin said with a twinkle in his eyes. Breaking into a whistle, he did a jig down the stairs.

The stunned housekeeper stood with her smile frozen in place. With a hand over her heart, she breathed, "My— my goodness, what can he mean by that?" Turning, she walked straight into the door of the linen closet.

The squire stood still for several minutes after he stepped into the barn to allow his eyes time to adjust from the dazzling light off the snow to the muted light within. He could hear Audacia singing, but instead of the usual lyrical joy this melody was filled with sadness. He noted happily that for all the lack of joy in the tune, her voice was clear and strong. The cold wetting had done her no harm. Geoffrey thought of Greydon and could not suppress a chuckle, for the earl had been even more miserable and irritable this morn.

The last words of the dirgelike ballad were faint in the air when Webster stepped noiselessly into the small area of the barn partitioned off for Audacia's "brood." Many animals stayed only a short time—until they had regained their strength or an injury healed. A miscellaneous assortment of birds, rabbits, even a wild fox now occupied the pens and cages. The longest tenant was the one Audacia was now bending over, a yearling deer that had been badly injured by a wild dog, probably the same one that was killing the squire's sheep.

Geoffrey watched as Audacia ran her hands gently over the trusting animal, adjusted the bandage, and rose. He walked forward, the crinkle of the straw beneath his boots startling Audacia, who had not heard him enter.

"Oh, Geoffrey," she cried, recognizing him. In an instant she had flown to his side, wrapping her arms about him.

Overcoming his shock at this greeting, he put his arm about her shoulders as she sobbed against his chest. When the outburst had calmed to sniffles, he said softly, attempting to humor her, "You had better use your kerchief or my cravat will be forever ruined."

Releasing her hold, Audacia dug into the pockets of the apron she wore over her burnt-orange day dress and withdrew a large, white kerchief.

"Blow hard," the squire admonished as he guided her to a bench against the wall. Sitting, he tugged on her hand until she sat beside him. "What has occurred to bring such a storm of tears, Audacia? It is most unlike you. Has one of your little ones died?" he asked, his eyes sweeping over the cages and small pens in the area.

Shaking her head, Audacia raised her tear-filled eyes to his. "I am . . . being . . . a . . . bloody coward," she managed between sniffles.

"You, a coward?" His hand kept her from turning from him. "I cannot imagine that. Why don't you tell me what troubles you so? It would please me greatly if I could be of aid to you this time."

"If only you could help," Audacia said lowly, then blew her nose vigorously and straightened her shoulders. "There is no help for me, though. Father has made up his mind and it cannot be altered. Oh, what am I to do?" she asked, so woebegone his heart wrenched. "Father is sending me to stay with Lord and Lady Darby, and they are to take me to London for the season."

A laugh broke from Geoffrey, which he tried to swallow when he saw Audacia's reaction.

"There is nothing amusing in this," she said sharply. "I do not see you agog to go to London each season."

"But I have a good reason for remaining here. You should be rejoicing to at last have a season like all the other young women you know. Many a young gir—woman," he amended quickly, "dreams of just such an opportunity. There will be balls, soirees, morning calls, afternoons in the park, shopping . . . ah, shopping as you have never seen. And you, you shall be noticed wherever you go," Webster ended, appreciation of Audacia's looks suddenly dawning. Roland is right, he thought, her eyes, glistening with tears, are like great sparkling diamonds.

"I do not care for dancing . . . or for any of that folderol. What do I care for shopping? Why you know I am not one for geegaws. What are you staring at?" she demanded, irritated that he was not seeing her part in this.

"You are in quite good looks this morn, Miss Aderly," Geoffrey answered lightly. "All the beaux and dandies will fall at your feet for the simple pleasure of a dance." With a teasing glint, he added, "Now what is it that is so different? Why I cannot decide."

Audacia blushed fiercely. "You know it is that I am in a gown today," she retorted, "and it is all your fault."

"Lord forbid I should dictate the dress of any female," he feigned shock. "How can your mode of toilet be laid to my head," the squire tossed back innocently.

"It is that—that oaf you have staying with you. I only hope he has taken a dreadful chill," she pouted.

"Vengeance is not your way, Audacia," Geoffrey frowned. "Why so harsh a feeling for a man you do not know?"

"There is just something about the man. His air of—of being a nonpareil, I suppose," she muttered.

"Well, he has taken a dreadful chill. I left him in his bed shivering like a wet pup, filled with fever and cough."

" 'Tis not like you to jest me thus," Audacia noted; her suspicion of the truth of his words was apparent.

"I have never told you a falsehood before and I do not now," he assured her. "The Earl of Greydon feels very miserable—thanks to you."

"The wretched man. Can he not even . . . ohh," she sighed. "Have you given him honey balm for the throat and cough? What of a plaster for his chest?" Audacia's words ended abruptly as a thought occurred. After a pause she asked, "Did you say the 'Earl of Greydon'?"

"Yes, his lordship, Roland, Earl of Greydon, heir to the Marquess of Mandel."

"Oh, dear, Father will be even more upset if he learns of this." She clasped and unclasped her hands.

"Why would Roland's rank be of note to your father?"

"Because," she began, then halted as she saw Geoffrey's telling grin. "You know, you do know all about it. Oh, he has told you and everyone. To hear Father such a happening is worse than if I had drowned. Can you tell me what is so scandalous about being rescued from drowning?" Audacia ended disgustedly.

"*Certe,* I do not wish you had drowned . . ."

"And I know Father does not either. But just explain what *is* so terrible about the event. When I question Father

60

he simply ahems until he's flush in the face and then disappears."

"So he has not told you what occurred after you were pulled from the river. I do not wonder at that, though."

"Happened? Nothing happened. I think you men should all be taken to Bedlam. You're all daft," she snapped and rose abruptly.

"Audacia, Roland thought you were a young lad. When he got you to Stollard's cottage he began to take off your wet garments so that you would not catch a chill, and he then learned you were not what he thought," the squire told her bluntly.

For a second Audacia simply stared. The words' meaning penetrated slowly; her cheeks flamed, then paled. She settled soundly back on the bench. "Father knows of this?" she breathed.

"He must. Why else would he be sending you to London? I imagine Mrs. Stollard told him, but Roland has spoken to no one and will not," Geoffrey assured her, patting her awkwardly on the shoulder.

"How could he do that?" Audacia breathed aloud to herself.

"Use your sense now; Roland saved your life. You seem to think he had a definite plan to compromise you. It was not his fault you could not let a water hen freeze. How was he to know you were a . . . woman," Geoffrey defended his friend. "In London it would be unthinkable for a female to appear in breeches."

"Here also it seems," Audacia said with a wry grin. "Oh, I did not mean to speak harshly of the earl. It must be that I am so angry with myself I cannot reason. He will mend?"

61

"Roland has the constitution of a draft horse. A chill will not keep him abed for long."

"Anyone who is as insufferable as he is couldn't become too ill," Audacia quipped. "Oh, there it is again. Why is it he sets my hackles up so? No one has ever had this effect on me before."

"I know not why, but do you recall how I was when we first met?" Geoffrey slowly asked her. "I was ill in body and spirit and had it not been for you I would have put an end to my life."

"What reason do you have for mentioning this now?" she asked, peering sharply at the squire for signs she may have missed in her self-concern.

"Do not stare so, I am fine," he assured her, "but Roland reminds me of how I was then in so many ways."

"But he has no signs of wounds. What reason would he have for . . . ?"

"It is a fact that neither bullet nor blade ever did serious damage, but his moods, his actions, some of the things he says are . . . so at odds with the man I knew before the war. If you would visit with him I know you would understand what I mean."

"Roland Greydon, that name seems strangely familiar. Greydon?" Recognition came. "He is the one who . . ." Her eyes went to the empty sleeve as she realized why he was of such importance to the squire.

"Yes, Audacia, he is the one."

"Audacia? Squire Webster?" Sir Aderly's voice reached their ears.

"Coming, Father," Audacia answered, rising. "Pretend to know nothing about yesterday. It will ease Father's mind so," she urged in a low tone.

Smiling, Geoffrey nodded and taking her hand led the way back to the main area of the barn.

"Good day, Sir Aderly. Miss Audacia was showing me how well the deer has progressed."

"Ahem, well, yes," Sir Maurice mumbled taking in the clasped hands of the two. "Well, come inside now. You could use some warm punch to take the chill from your bones after your ride here."

"That would be appreciated. Mayhaps I could also see how your work progresses," Geoffrey noted.

"Always happy to do that, my boy," Sir Maurice returned brightly. "Where is your cloak, Audacia?" he asked, seeing none close at hand.

"I left it with the animals. Wait a moment and I will fetch it."

With his daughter out of sight, Sir Aderly edged closer to Squire Webster and asked, "Have you heard of any London dandies or fops visiting anyone in our area?"

"Dandies? Why no, sir, although the Earl of Greydon is staying with me. He came to rest and relax and is now abed, having taken a chill," Webster returned, managing a straight face.

"Abed, you say? No harm there," he said distractedly. "Oh, too bad about your friend. Hope the chill is of short duration. But tell me, have you heard of any . . . gossip of late?"

"Nothing unusual, sir. Is there something I should know of?"

"No. No. Here you are, Audacia. Let us return to the house. Squire Webster and I can look over my work and you can help Miss Strowne with the packing. I have decided you are to leave on the morrow," Sir Maurice told her, taking advantage of the squire's presence to impart the news.

"On the morrow?! Father, please . . ."

"You know you shall enjoy your visit, Audacia. We must not bore the squire with family matters." He turned to Webster and asked, "Do you know of the Darbys, from Worcester?"

"I have not been to London, except for matters of business, for over five years," Geoffrey answered, ignoring Audacia's grimace. "Therefore I do not know many of the gentry who attend the season. The name does seem to ring familiar though."

"When Lady Aderly and I were in London, the Darbys were very popular. I imagine it is the same now. But come, I have added a pulley which may solve the problem with . . ."

Audacia walked slowly before the two men toward the house, their conversation a mumble of sounds to her ears. The morrow would come swiftly, she knew, and the thought of leaving her home was a heavy weight on her heart.

And Geoffrey's friend, she thought with a strain of regret, I will not meet him now. But I only wanted to become acquainted with him because of Geoffrey, she assured herself, only to blush fiercely as she recalled the squire's words about what had occurred after her rescue. What *would* I do if ever I did meet him? she asked herself, her cheeks hot in the cold winter air. Even as she wondered, the regret persisted. Reaching the house, Audacia pushed this ruing she could not understand from her mind and gathered courage for her coming journey.

64

CHAPTER VII

Having bid Audacia a somber farewell, Squire Webster rode leisurely toward Web Manor. Many conflicting thoughts crowded his mind in confusion. He wished to sort through them all before speaking with Greydon again.

Roland's brief mention of his sister on the eve before had evoked the full storm of emotions Geoffrey had finally forced to the shadows of his mind after much struggle. He now had to battle through the pain of rejected love once more, and it was as if it were yesterday. That last awkward, heartrending interview with Lady Lucille in London seven years past.

"The Honorable Lieutenant Webster," the Mandels' butler announced to the two women in the sitting room, stepping aside to allow the gaunt, red-coated gentleman to enter.

"Geoffrey, how good to see you looking . . . so improved." Lady Mandel rose with a smile.

He nodded greeting, his features taut with tension, his eyes begging the young lady still seated beside her mother to meet his gaze.

"Do forgive me, I have just recalled I neglected to give cook the menu for this eve," Lady Mandel said. "I will return shortly."

Lady Lucille fretfully twisted the white ribbon at her tiny waist, her look imploring her mother to take pity and remain.

Webster nodded his gratitude for the privacy she was granting them. He swallowed hard when her ladyship paused at his side and gave his remaining arm a consoling squeeze. "She is so very young," she whispered as if to apologize and was gone.

"Will you not look at me, Lucille?" Webster broke the heavy silence, his voice weighted with resignation.

"Of—of course." Her eyes flitted to his, winced at the concealed stub of arm, and hastened to her hands. "I—I— oh, do sit, Geoffrey," her voice rose in panic as he wavered.

" 'Tis nothing," he assured her but sank to the settee with relief. "Cursed weakness from the . . . operation. The doctors say it will pass now that the infection is gone."

"It—it is healing, then." She fidgeted with the cameo lying against her white throat.

"Yes. I mean to return to Web Manor on the morrow." He studied her light brown curls caught by a bright blue ribbon, which matched her gown, and memorized how they framed her delicate oval face.

"Oh, good . . . oh." Red tinged Lady Lucille's pale

cheeks. "I did not mean . . . I, that is, the air is so much better in the country," she ended feebly.

"I thought we should speak of our betrothal before I departed." The lieutenant's shoulders squared; his resolve to carry through his decision was stiffened by her relief at his leaving London.

Lady Lucille jumped up, her agitation poorly concealed. "Yes, I suppose we must." Her hands gripped each other tightly and she walked to the fireplace. "Shall a date be set as soon as you regain your strength?"

"I love you, Lucille." Geoffrey's voice cracked over the softly spoken words. He held out his hand.

She turned slowly, steeling herself. "I promised to wed you and I shall."

The lieutenant gulped back sudden tears welling in his throat, silently cursing his weakness. Her look, her words confirmed his worst fears and he slowly drew back his hand. He could not endure seeing that pity every day for the rest of his life, nor risk it turning to hate. Rising unsteadily, Webster walked slowly to her.

Lady Lucille stiffened at his approach but allowed him to caress her cheek.

Geoffrey tenderly brushed her forehead with a kiss then turned abruptly away. "Do you love me, Lucille?"

"Why . . . yes. Of course . . . I did . . . I must." Tears sprang to her eyes as he faced her. "I am so sorry, Geoffrey," she reached out but he shook his head.

"I think it best that your father announce our betrothal is ended."

"No, we must not . . ."

"We must not make each other more wretched than we now are." Webster regained control of his emotions. "I

67

will send a letter to him explaining. He will understand. You need fear no embarrassment. I shall remain in Warwickshire . . . indefinitely."

Lady Lucille opened her mouth to speak but no words came. Confusion rioted in her heart. Of late she had thought it would be a joy to be freed from their betrothal but now only a dull ache filled her. He looked so brave; she blinked back tears recalling how gay and handsome Geoffrey was the day they had bid each other farewell, vowing never-ending love. How she had hungered to have his arms remain about her that day and now . . . "Give me time, Geoffrey." The words sprang forth unbidden. "I will become accustomed . . ." Her voice trailed away in uncertainty.

"I was highly honored to have been your betrothed." Geoffrey bowed stiffly. "I wish you happiness." He turned on his heel and walked swiftly away.

God, how beautiful she was! The squire forced his mind back to the present, back to Audacia. Yes, Roland had opened his eyes concerning her. Suddenly, he saw Audacia for the beautiful young woman she was, not merely the comfortable friend who'd helped him through a difficult time. Her coming-out in London caused him much concern. Could a young woman as mischievous as she, with no mother to guide her, survive the rigors of the "season"? Would she withstand the dowagers' inspection? Could she handle the young dandies and the rakes who would certainly pursue her?

And what was to be made of Roland? Obviously something was lying heavy upon the man's mind.

When he arrived home, Steins, the butler, opened the

door before Webster reached it. "Squire, thanks be for your return. His lordship has been asking of you rather frequently for the hour past," the harassed man greeted his master. "Could you see him?"

"I'll go right up, Steins. Have a light collation prepared for my lunch and some broth for his lordship. Bring both to his chambers, we shall dine there," the squire instructed as he handed his hat, coat, and glove to the man. With slow steps, he mounted the stairs and paused outside Greydon's door. A moment of concentration pushed his concerns aside and he strode into the bedchamber with a light smile upon his lips.

Greydon, who had been leafing fretfully through a book, tossed it aside, folded his arms, and glared expectantly.

Nodding a greeting, Geoffrey retrieved the book from the edge of the bed. Opening it, his eyes fell on a passage. Giving a wide grin he read, " 'Shall I compare thee to a summer's day?

Thou art more lovely and more temperate.' Now to my mind you look more like an October storm." Geoffrey laughed, closing the book. "Shakespeare, my friend? A good companion, indeed. I could not offer you better for improving your mind. But if you wish to keep abreast of your social whirl perhaps I could have Steins bring the *Gazette* to you after lunch."

"Brought to me. Bah!" Greydon scoffed. "I am no puling child to be waited upon at every turn. Would you have me a cripple?"

"Even cripples have their uses," Geoffrey noted gently, then regretted his words at his friend's look of dismay. "Taking care now and lying abed but a day or two is far better than misusing your health and lying abed a month," he hurried to say. Tossing the book back to the earl, he noted, "My ride was invigorating. It is a damnable inconvenience that you could not attend with me. Miss Aderly wished you dire health, but immediately regretted it and began insisting upon preparing a poultice for your chest. A desire for retribution perhaps?" he asked. Raising his voice above Greydon's answering growl, he added, "But never fear. I have saved you from the prospect of having to bare your anatomy."

"Doing it too brown, Geoff," Greydon said tersely. "Miss Aderly was very decently covered by her chemise."

"I did not ask, but then, Audacia may wish to question you about that." Webster smiled. "She had no idea why her father was . . . er, 'upset' about the situation."

"And you enlightened her? You bloody fool," the earl cursed, pushing aside the bedcovers and making to get out of the bed. The quick movement brought on light-headedness and he was forced to lie back. "When I am recovered you shall make restitution for your loose tongue."

"My loose tongue? But I was the spirit of discretion. I even managed to fob off Sir Aderly rather well."

"Fob Aderly off? About what?" Greydon questioned suspiciously.

"He inquired if I knew of any dandies or fops visiting in the area," Webster said, taking a seat in the chair by the fireplace, "and I did rather well assuring him I knew of none despite your presence here."

A scowl curled Greydon's lips then departed. "Then Miss Aderly is well?" he asked, voicing his thought.

"In the best of health."

"What did you learn from Aderly? Does he consider her honor impugned?"

"I know not. It seems you rescued the wrong person, my lord. If you questioned the baronet I am certain he would insist his man's nephew, who supposedly happens to be visiting, was rescued by some gentleman who is strange to the area." Geoffrey watched the earl's reaction to this news. His friend's continuing interest, even concern, for someone of Audacia's sort was extraordinary.

"The man had best see to his daughter. I wonder if he knows how fortunate he was that someone like that Darby fop didn't come along. Did you learn what steps he means to take with her?"

"What name was that you mentioned?" the squire asked, disregarding the earl's questions.

"Name? You mean Darby's? I heard gossip of him before I left London."

"What was it you heard?"

"According to the 'ladies' who spoke of him he is a comely lad. Their latest on-dit was that his gaming losses were more than his father could cover. More titillating for the ladies was the rumor that he had stayed at the home of one of his father's friends and, well, let us say it was about a young daughter of the friend. The insinuation was quashed but most dowagers are now wise enough to keep their daughters from his way."

"Is he of the Worcester Darbys?" Geoffrey asked, now seated at the edge of his chair.

"There are no others remaining of the family but the Worcester branch. But enough of gossip. What is to be done with Miss Aderly?" he persisted.

"In the morn Audacia is being sent to Lord and Lady

Darby at Worcester. They are to sponsor her this season," Geoffrey answered tersely, his brow furrowed with concern.

"Is the man a fool? Has he no care for his daughter? How can he send her to them knowing what the son is?" Greydon asked in disbelief.

"Lady Darby was a close friend of Lady Aderly. I gather that she promised to take Audacia in hand when she came of age when that good lady died. Besides, Aderly is not much in London, nor does he peer over the puffs in the *Gazette*. His only interest is in his machines. I daresay he still believes the Darbys to be among the best of the quality. He asked me if I had heard of them of late but of course I had no idea . . . Damme," the squire cursed, "I have already said I know nothing of the Darbys. I cannot go to Aderly without revealing this conversation, and what could I say if he asked why we were discussing his daughter? He's no slow top. Could start asking more damning questions. What's to be done?"

"What's the chit to you that your hackles are raised so?" Greydon asked, eyeing his friend closely.

"A friend, a damned good friend, and a lamb when it comes to Darby's sort. I told you before that I would not see harm done her."

"If you're so keen on the wench, why don't you offer for her," the earl returned, with more spirit than he meant to use.

"That I may," Geoffrey threw back, rising. "She is as fine a woman as there is to be found in the kingdom."

"There is no need for such extreme measures, yet," Greydon retorted a bit hastily. "Darby was sent to Cornwall to rusticate."

"Why did you not tell me that from the first?"

"I wasn't asked."

"Your pardon, my lord . . . your honor." Stein's quiet voice made the two men realize they had been shouting. "Shall I serve you now?"

"I should like to dine alone," Greydon told him.

"Very well, my lord," Webster made a mock bow. "Bring my lunch to the library, Steins," he ordered and stalked out of the chamber.

Greydon accepted his tray and waved the butler and his valet, who had entered behind the other, out of the chamber. Picking up his spoon, he tasted the broth, but it aroused no interest. Dropping the spoon disgustedly into the bowl, he lay back and closed his eyes. Immediately he saw Audacia, wrapped in the woolen blanket, seated before the cottage's fireplace. The black velvet of her half-dried hair framed her sturdy face. He longed to reach out and feel the softness of that black wealth, to look deep into those constantly changing, challenging eyes.

With a start, Greydon shook himself. "Want to make a bloody fool of yourself," he muttered. What is it about the chit that makes me moon like a green youth over a first love. I know her not. Anger mingled with his strange yearning to know more of the girl, for Geoffrey had shown a particular interest and Greydon was determined none of his family would ever again be the cause of pain to his friend.

A few bites of food from his plate were enough for Geoffrey and he pushed it away. Why did I lose my temper with Roland? he asked himself. His curiosity about

Audacia bothers me not. Then what? The squire rose and began pacing.

That Roland can be drawn to shouting is a certain sign of his interest in Audacia, Geoffrey thought, and I bungled the handling of that. Pausing before the windows, he saw his one-armed reflection and cursed. "That's it, fool. Look at yourself." Mayhaps Roland is not far from the mark, he thought. Audacia would make an excellent wife for me. She has never looked at me with pity like some. "Oh, God," Geoffrey moaned and turned from the window. That's why I was angry. Why didn't it come to me before. The only way to help Audacia is to go to London, and if I do that I cannot help but see Lucille and that look of pity that has been a haunting spectre these last years. So it has come at last, he thought bitterly. Now you have no choice but to face it through.

"Is your packing completed, daughter?" Sir Maurice asked when Audacia came to his workroom to bid him good night.

"Yes, Father, there was not much to be taken. My gowns will be frightfully out of style."

"Do not fear for that. I have attended the matter. It is one of the reasons I wish you to leave so early. Lady Darby will be a much better guide in selecting the proper fashions than I, and so I have prepared letters for her explaining what I wish and also a draft for you from which you may draw for pin money. Buy all the furbelows and geegaws you like. Remember, you are to enjoy yourself," he told her as he turned his cheek for her kiss.

Audacia nodded, totally unconvinced that enjoyment

could be found in the purchase of anything as farcical as geegaws.

"You may even encounter your brother in London," Sir Aderly noted, trying to hearten her.

"Daniel?"

"What other? He wrote and asked if he might go with Viscount Hillern and a friend. I received his letter just yesterday and will write on the morrow granting my permission if you wish."

"Oh, Father," Audacia gave him a crushing hug. "That would be absolutely marvelous!"

"Fine then. Now off with you. We shall be rising early. The mail coach will be halting at the crossing by six and we must be there. Mr. Ballin and I shall drive you and Miss Strowne."

"Could you not come to London, Father? Then there would be no need for my going to the Darbys," Audacia asked hopefully.

"I may, I may. We shall see. But you must go, for as I said, gowns and frills are not for me to choose. Sleep well."

Abed a short while later, Audacia found that sleep came quickly, but with it came wild, odd dreams of Daniel and Geoffrey, with Earl Greydon ever in the shadow of their steps.

CHAPTER VIII

Audacia looked uneasily to Miss Bea when the stern-faced butler at Lord Darby's said she should follow him. Alone. The past three days had been filled with eye-widening sights for the young woman, who could not remember her only journey to her home near Bedworth. More than once during the days of bone-jarring, flesh-chilling, body-bruising travel, she had been thankful for Miss Bea's steadying, reassuring presence. Having reached Malvern by late afternoon, the pair had hired a post chaise and arrived at the Darby estate after sunset, where they hoped for quiet and rest.

The sight of the huge Gothic mansion, shadowed against the moonlit sky, had proven more chilling than comforting. The mounted gargoyles and myriad reflecting windowpanes reminded her of staring eyes. There was no feeling of welcoming warmth to be found. Even the park they drove through to reach the main entrance of the house was filled with bare-branched shadowy shrubs, which brought her father's fearful tales of haunting spirits to mind.

When they had stepped from the coach, Audacia had glanced up at the stretch of overgrown ivy, which was reaching out like a cloak to cover the windows, and resolved not to be separated from Miss Bea.

"Miss?" the stiff-faced butler called, turning to see that the young woman was hesitant to leave her companion. "Your woman will be seen to. We must not keep her ladyship waiting," he clipped impatiently.

"Of—of course," Audacia answered unsteadily, unaccustomed to so abrupt a manner. She brushed at her wrinkled and worn pelisse, attempting to smooth some of the travel creases from it as she followed his steps.

The great corridor the butler led her through was as wide as the morning room at home and Audacia was agog at it, and at the golden candelabras mounted on the linen-fold paneled walls. Only a few stubby candles burned in these instead of the full complement, and Audacia could only wish for more light with which to examine the wonders that appeared as they progressed.

Passing a full suit of armor standing with jousting staff in the metal gauntlet, she was reminded of tales of knights of old and wondered if some member of the family long ago had been a true gallant. A richly colored woven tapestry of an Elizabethan court scene caught her eye, and its value reminded her of the wealth of her mother's friend. So absorbed was she in the court scene that it was not until she had walked squarely into the butler that Audacia realized he had halted and opened a door, awaiting her to enter.

"Oh, my," she stammered, righting herself and reaching to straighten her poke bonnet. Miss Bea's admonition never to apologize to servants rang in her ears as she saw the look of glowering disapproval. Her eyes lowered quickly from his, and with a sinking heart she entered the large chamber alone.

A parsimonious fire flickered in the massive fireplace. An unnecessary fire screen of oriental design, much like one that Audacia had read about the Prince of Wales having at Brighton, stood behind a chair. A small table was placed next to the fire. Seated in a chair near this table, bent over an embroidery hoop before her, sat a large-nosed, stern-faced woman who looked to be of Sir Aderly's age. Though she was robed in a faultless empire gown, the lady's plumpness defeated the dress's intended decorative effect.

Audacia took heart and strode purposefully toward the woman, halting just a few steps away. Her foot began tapping and she clasped her hands behind her back as the woman paid no attention to her. "My lady," she ventured finally.

"I shall address you when I see fit, young lady," Lady Darby answered, her rounded shoulders remaining bent over her stitching. "Be silent till spoken to."

With a deep frown, Audacia glanced about the room. It was in the shape of a huge square, so large that the light from the fireplace was far too meager for her to make out much of its contents. The fireplace itself was surrounded by an exquisitely rendered series of carved biblical scenes.

"Now, miss—I take it you are Miss Aderly," Lady Darby said slowly, raising her eyes to inspect the figure before her.

Warmth rose to Audacia's cheeks at this blatant scrutiny. Resentment flared then waned as a wave of fatigue swept over her and she tried to stifle a yawn.

"You may stay the evening . . . and perhaps one other day. It could be pleasant to reminisce about your mother, I suppose. But, my dear, your father misunderstood my intent in regard to you," the viscountess said coldly, cocking her head as she assessed Audacia's form.

"My father asked that I give these to you upon my arrival," Audacia told the woman tonelessly, wishing to end the interview and be allowed to retire. Withdrawing the sealed letters and money drafts from her reticule, she handed them over.

The letters, unopened, were tossed casually atop the table. The bank drafts, however, were greedily scanned, and a bright smile came over the woman's face as she stared at first one, then the other. "Why you must be exhausted," she crooned, rising. "How unkind of me to keep you standing in this chilled room." She pulled the bell cord, retrieved the letters, and then put an arm around Audacia's shoulders and guided her toward the door. "It was such a charming letter I had from your father," she twittered, her chin wriggling comically. "Why, we had forgotten you would be of such an age. The years pass too quickly do they not? How does your father fare? Oh, here is Trotter. He shall take you to the Green Room. It has a small antechamber. You did bring an abigail? Your father had mentioned that you would?"

"Yes, my lady," Audacia replied, wishing Lady Darby would not stay quite so near.

"She can sleep in that small chamber. It will be quite comfortable. Would that please you?" she gurgled. "When you are rested in the morn we can talk about plans," the viscountess continued without pausing to let Audacia speak. "Take Miss Aderly by way of the solarium, Trotter. The Green Room," she ordered with a curt nod. "Sleep well, my dear."

Too tired to delve into the reasons behind Lady Darby's sudden change in attitude, Audacia curtsied tiredly and followed the butler, thankful to be allowed to retire for the evening. "Plans," as Lady Darby said, could be laid in the morn.

With Trotter leading her unbidden guest from sight, Lady Darby took the skirt of her high-waisted gown in hand and hurried down the hall. A hard yank on the first bell cord she came to produced the housekeeper and one of the maids. "To the Green Room, both of you. Get the dust covers off the furniture and be quick about it. Trotter is taking Miss Aderly there but will go through the solarium first. Where is the abigail?"

"In the kitchen, my lady," replied the wizened housekeeper, Mrs. Scrannot.

"Send her and a footman to manage their baggage. You should be finished in the room before they reach it."

"Of course, my lady."

Turning from the servants, Lady Darby twittered gleefully as she hurried towards her husband's chambers.

"I thought the Aderly miss wasn't to stay," the maid spoke lowly to the housekeeper as they began the long flight of stairs to the upper floor.

"It is not yours to question her ladyship. The Green Room is large and there are many pieces of furniture to be uncovered."

"I thought the Green Room was to be kept for her

80

ladyship's high-stepping friends from London," the maid continued to gossip. "Not that we've seen many of those of late."

"Lady Darby has not seen the need for much company of late," Mrs. Scrannot said defensively.

"But there was a time when the house overflowed with them fancy dressin' women and the free-handed men. Can't help but wonder . . ."

"You are not paid to wonder about anything her ladyship does," the housekeeper admonished.

"Aye, true that is. One does get to thinkin' about pay. I keep hearin' rumors that the merchants at Malvern are highly unhappy with his lordship," Mrs. Black continued to prattle.

"You have been here long enough to know to ignore such hearsay," Mrs. Scrannot advised, torn between loyalty to the family and a desire to know what was being bandied about. "If we tarry, the young miss will arrive before we are finished . . ."

"Aye, and then her ladyship would have reason to dismiss us," the maid remarked scornfully, and hastened her steps.

The Honorable Mr. Patrick Darby, consigned to visit a friend in a rather desolate section of Cornwall, had welcomed the appearance of another friend, the viscount Hillern, and the two of them had, on this eve, outlasted their host. Drink had not only rendered their host senseless but had also loosened young Darby's tongue as he and Hillern enjoyed reminiscences of their more lascivious deeds of the past. Being deep in his cups, the viscount's mind wandered and he abruptly said. "This place is absolutely revolting." Grabbing at the near-empty bottle of port, the sixth of the evening, he added, "I refuse to remain here beyond the morrow."

"Lucky you are that you are free to go. You have only arrived the day just past," Darby told him, "and I have been here an eternity." His sallow complexion, reddened by drink, darkened. "There's naught to do but eat and drink." He waved a hand and dropped it to his pettishly plump waist, "Damn this place."

Hillern raised his glass in answer and burst into raucous-laughter. "Your lesson has been learned then? Discretion, my boy, discretion."

"I'll not take offense," Darby said pompously then demanded, "have you received a reply?"

"Reply? Oh, from the Aderly chap. No, but I see no problem with it. Aderly could be convinced to come whether his father approves or not." The viscount drank deeply. "Do you really think your scheme will succeed?"

"My skill is not unknown to you, Hillern. Mother shall be convinced I have been utterly reformed if Aderly is as green, as gullible as you say."

"There is none greener. Won't even go near the muslin set," Hillern smirked.

"Then we shall have to give the lad our reckoning of the 'grand tour' when we arrive in London. The least I can do for anyone helping free me of the damnable place." Darby threw his glass against the wall in disgust. "Send word to me as soon as you hear from him. My properly contrite letters have been preparing mother for my return. Bringing Aderly with me should prove the proper balm. Once forgiven there is need only of one run of luck . . ."

"Or a willing heiress," Hillern threw in, drink making him uncautious with his friend.

A scowl covered Darby's plump looks, removing any hint of pleasantness from his features. "Mother needs little prodding there. I find it remarkable that she has not summoned me home to meet her latest 'protege.' I am not unwilling," he swaggered back in his chair, "provided there are funds worth the taking. In all, though, I prefer the die or cards. I feel my luck has changed," he leaned forward, a grimness about him. "Fortune is about to smile on me, Hillern. I can feel it."

"The smell of dust is in the air. In the morn when there is some light you shall see it all about," Miss Bea groused as she unpacked Audacia's few garments. "A household of this size and only two candles, hruummph."

"Lady Darby is a rather odd woman," Audacia murmured as she undressed. "At first I thought we might be told to leave. It seemed as if she was very unhappy about our coming. But," she said as she sighed tiredly, "she was almost too welcoming after I gave her father's letters."

"As weary as you are you may have imagined she was cool towards you."

Audacia shrugged, then pulled her nightdress over her head.

Miss Bea yawned widely.

"But couldn't I help you? You must be as exhausted as I."

"That is no way for a young lady to speak. You must always act as if you expect to be waited upon. Demand it, in fact."

"I shall never become accustomed to it, Miss Bea," Audacia said tiredly.

"And be careful of how you address me. Miss Bea is fine for moments when we are alone but if anyone is about you must simply say 'Strowne, do this.' I'll have none of these servants running to her ladyship with tales that you behave improperly."

"But I care not for what any one of them thinks."

"Then you must begin now. We are going to do this properly. I've my pride and no one is going to say I am not a suitable abigail. To bed with you. I want you rested and in the best of looks in the morn. The light of day will raise your spirits."

Climbing into the broad feather bed, Audacia told Miss Bea, "You sound more a nanny than an abigail to my ears."

"All the more reason for you to take care with your words and actions," Miss Strowne admonished, coming to the bedside to straighten the bedcovers.

"You haven't done this for years, Miss Bea," Audacia said, tears suddenly welling in her eyes. "Thank you, for coming with me and—and everything."

" 'Tis nothing, child," the pseudo-abigail told her with a shaking voice, "but you must see I am properly rewarded by making the best match of the season." Miss Bea raised her head proudly. "Your mother was a beauty, no less are you. The man you accept will have the kindest, truest wife in the kingdom." She blew her nose noisily and gazed down at the young woman who was half smiling at her words. "And the most mischievous, prank-filled miss ever to come his way," she added with false anger before turning away.

A gurgle of laughter came from Audacia in answer as she turned onto her stomach. The one thing she was most certain this trip did *not* hold in store for her was a husband.

CHAPTER IX

"Why, miss, you should still be abed," Miss Bea scolded when she came from the small antechamber and found Audacia gazing out of the sun-streaked windows.

"It would probably be warmer there," Audacia said turning from the windows. "But it must be after ten and my stomach has been protesting the lack of food since eight."

"A lady's stomach does nothing of the sort."

"If ladies are permitted such a vulgar organ," Audacia mimicked.

"Young lady." The abigail straightened herself stiffly.

"Oh, I know, Miss Bea. But my stomach hasn't learned of its gentility yet," she said and burst into laughter.

The older woman tried her best to frown but the absurdity was too apparent. Feeling her cause lost for the moment, she took to new ground. "Why, look at those windows. They have not been washed for a sennight of months," she ejaculated, seeing that the bright sunshine shadowed through the streaked, begrimed panes. "And look, there is dust all about."

"I do not believe her ladyship intended this room for us," Audacia noted. "Something caused her to change her mind. What could it have been?"

"Lady Darby must not be careful about the servants she employs. Why this room looks as if it has been neglected completely; as if the dustcovers have just been taken from it."

"What of the lack of a fire? I was tempted to use those chairs by the fireplace for firewood," Audacia quipped. "Never have I been so thoroughly chilled."

"One must question the lack of amenities," Miss Bea began hesitantly. "I do hope Sir Aderly was not wrong in thinking the viscount still among the ton."

"It would be a pleasure to learn they are not, for then we could return home. But if I do not find sustenance soon I shall be too weak to even stand." Audacia drew her hand to her forehead, feigned light-headedness, and staggered theatrically.

"Miss, you had best watch out for the—" Before the abigail could complete her warning, the young woman caught her heel on a chair and stumbled against the wall.

Catching hold the wide, fringed cord nearby, she righted herself. "I had thought this a rather useless decoration," she said giving it another tug.

Both women started in surprise as the door burst open and a worried looking maid bolted to the center of the room and fell into a deep curtsy. "Yes, milady," she huffed through hard-drawn breaths.

"What is the matter?" Audacia asked. "Why have you

been running?" She looked to the door to see if the maid had been pursued.

"I came—as—quickly—as I could, milady," the plump young woman panted.

"I am simply Miss Aderly," Audacia told her kindly. "Have you been frightened?"

"Why, no . . . miss. It is just that . . . well . . . you did give the bell a frightful pull," the maid explained hesitantly.

"The bell?" Audacia looked to Miss Bea, who nodded at the cord. "Oh, yes, the bell," she said turning back to the maid. "We were, that is, I was thinking I would like a light breakfast."

"Her ladyship instructed me to ask that you join his lordship and herself whenever you arose. I will show you to the breakfast room if you wish."

"That would be fine, but what of . . . Strowne?"

"I'll return and take her below stairs, miss. The breakfast room is this way."

Miss Bea walked with Audacia to the door. "Now remember a *light* breakfast," she whispered and crossed her fingers behind her back as Audacia's lively steps took the young woman from sight.

"Miss Aderly, what a pleasant surprise," Lord Darby greeted her entry into the breakfast room. He drew up his tall, thin frame to a stiffly upright posture as he said, "I had thought fatigue would delay your rising. But you are—my, yes," the graying viscount surveyed her with his quizzing glass, "—you *are* in the best of form." Having managed to reach her side, he took her hand and exclaimed, "Why, you are cold as ice. Was the fire in your room allowed to burn low?"

"There was no fire, my lord," Audacia answered, loosening the blue woolen shawl as she absorbed some of the warmth in the cosy room.

"No fire. Why who is responsible for this?" He turned to his wife. "Dismiss the wench who neglected her duty so badly," the viscount blustered.

"Of course, my lord," Lady Darby smiled innocently. "Be seated Miss Aderly—Audacia, is it not?" she twittered. "Such an unusual name, but then your father was rather odd. But come," she continued, heedless of the displeased glint in Audacia's eyes. "You must be famished after the journey and all, but I forget. Such excitement takes the appetite, does it not? Some chocolate? Perhaps a biscuit?"

Taking her seat, Audacia looked at the meager fare upon the table and tried to still the rumblings of her stomach that arose at the thought of one of Miss Bea's omelettes.

"My dear, we cannot tell you how pleasant it is to have you come and stay with us," the viscount told her. "You are quite like your mother in looks. A true beauty she was."

"Ahem," interrupted Lady Darby, throwing an annoyed frown at her husband. "Miss Aderly and I have much to discuss." She looked at Audacia. "Your father has asked that I see to all that is necessary for a successful season, and of course we know where to begin." She preened, adjusting the ruffles at the neck of her high-waisted brocade gown. When no compliment was forthcoming she hurried on. "There is a seamstress in Malvern that is quite good. We shall begin there for you *cannot* be seen in London in that"—she waved her hand languidly at Audacia's out-of-fashion daydress—"gown." Condemnation fell heavy with her words, and Audacia bristled. "I have ordered the coach for later in the afternoon. I had no idea your constitution was so, er, sound."

"I shall not mind the wait," Audacia broke in. "Would it be possible for me to walk about the grounds before we go?"

"Walk about the grounds? My dear, you surely do not mean to go outdoors?" Lord Darby asked, taken aback at the thought. "The gallery is—"

"I oft walk in the fresh air. I find it very beneficial," she broke in, giving the elderly man a wide smile.

"That is most unwise," Lady Darby intoned. "Exercise should be taken in moderation only. You could catch a dreadful chill. The gallery on the third floor is much more suitable for walking this time of year."

"Be assured that I am accustomed to the cold," Audacia told her happily. "May I have your permission?"

Lady Darby's attempt to conceal her displeasure failed, even though she gaily twittered, "Of course, dear girl, if you insist."

"Thank you, my lady. I think I shall go out now," Audacia said, finishing her chocolate. "Would it be possible to have tea when I come in?"

"You have only to express your desires, my dear," the viscount said, rising stiffly.

"There is no need. Please remain seated, my lord," she told him.

"Trotter." Lady Darby motioned the butler, who had been standing at the door since Audacia had entered, to

90

come forward. "See that Miss Aderly is shown the gardens."

The butler bowed formally at both Lord and Lady Darby, then led the way from the room. He did not stop until he stood before two huge doors at the end of one of the mansion's wings.

"Must I use these doors, Mr. Trotter?" Audacia asked the impervious-looking butler. "Are there no other . . . smaller doors, perhaps?"

"There is an entrance to the gardens not far from the library but it is used by the servants, miss," he answered stonily.

"Show me it, please. I am certain it shall be more suitable to my purpose." And far easier to open by myself, she thought looking at the massive doors, wondering if she could open them alone.

"As you wish," Trotter responded and they began a second trek back through the confusing corridors.

When they had passed the breakfast room, Audacia, determined to learn her way about, took her bearings. A sudden turn brought them to the most unusual corridor she had ever seen. Both sides were lined by what appeared to be door after identical door.

"The fifth viscount Darby was responsible for this ornamentation," Trotter announced proudly. "It is rather interesting. A very close examination will reveal which of the panels are true doors."

Surely he is not going to expect me to do that? she wondered in alarm. His next words brought relief.

"One enters the library through this." Trotter touched one of the panels lightly and it swung open. "Or through this one." Stepping four panels down the wall, he opened a second door. "But to enter the gardens, you must use this." He strode across the corridor and pushed the molding on one of the panels.

Audacia walked forward slowly. She shivered as she peered into the chilling darkness.

"A short tunnel, miss. The family does not use this exit but it is convenient for the servants."

"I—I am certain it will suit. If you could direct me to my room . . ."

"Of course, miss," he answered haughtily, thinking the young woman would now think twice before going outdoors.

After closing the door, he led the way back to the main corridor. A glance back would have shown him the young miss was far from deterred as she counted the number of "doors" between the real one and the end of the corridor.

Snow covered much of the gardens, but melting was clearly beginning and the slush underfoot bespoke the coming arrival of spring. Audacia made a wide circle around the outer limits several times before treading toward the center, where small hedge and shrubbery had caught the snow, increasing its depth. It was evident that none of the Darby household was interested in exercising in the open air, for only rabbit, squirrel, and bird tracks were visible across the white blanket. Recognizing the form of a bench beneath the snow, Audacia brushed vigorously until an area large enough for her to sit on was cleared. She sat and sighed as she looked at the tall walls of the mansion rising on two sides. A heavy sadness came upon her and she felt a deep longing to see her own, small home.

Audacia gasped the next instant as a snowball landed squarely on her back with a resounding thud. She whirled about and a second caught her in the face. Her gloved hand cleared the white crystals from her eyes just in time for her to see a third snowy missile and duck it. Her assailant, a girl of about four and ten, bent to scoop more snow in hand and on straightening received a blast of snow from Audacia's well-aimed throw.

The two eagerly exchanged blow for white blow until an angry, shrill voice called out. "Helene Darby, stop that vulgar behavior at once! And you, also, whoever you are. Come to me this instant." The window on the second floor slammed shut but Lady Darby's figure remained before it.

Slowly the two figures brushed snow from their pelisses and straightened their bonnets as they trudged towards the two large doors that Trotter had opened and was waiting before. Their steps joined reluctantly midway to the doors.

"I could have beaten you," Helene said hotly, her full face flushed.

"We will have to come out and try again." Audacia laughed as she spoke. "I have not had such fun since Daniel was sent off to school."

"Ohhhh," the young girl shook her head angrily.

Pausing, Audacia saw the loneliness behind the anger in the wide brown eyes. "My name is Audacia Aderly," she introduced herself. "I hope we can be friends during my stay."

"Friends?" Helene sneered, momentarily taking on her mothers' looks. "Why should I want to be friends with the daughter of a mere baronet? Here I am to suffer a scold from Mother and you have not the grace to fly into the boughs," she said disgustedly.

Audacia cast a knowing look at the younger girl. "What do you think Trotter would do if a snowball accidentally hit him?" she whispered conspiratorially.

The disgruntled expression upon the young girl's face melted into an appreciative smile, giving it a comely cast.

"But not now," Audacia cautioned. "Later . . .. Friend?"

Helene took a new assessment of her companion. 'Friend."

"Helene, I have told you I will not tolerate such abominable behavior," Lady Darby's scorching voice began as soon as the pair entered her sitting room. "Why, Miss Aderly—I cannot believe . . . Why . . ."

"Helene was simply enjoying a winter romp. Even I felt the need after the journey," Audacia told her calmly.

"But young lady." Lady Darby bit her lip.

"I apologize, my lady," Audacia said, giving the viscountess a low curtsy. "I could not see the harm here in these comfortable surroundings. Please pardon me for drawing Helene into such unladylike conduct," she said with the proper contrite tone and winked at the young girl, who was staring with admiration clearly apparent at such bold handling of her mother.

"Of course, we are in the country and—and you are not accustomed to our more formal ways. We must see to your instruction before we leave for London."

"Yes, my lady," she answered meekly.

"Well, then . . . both of you off to your rooms and change to dry garments. We leave for Malvern as soon as you are ready. Hurry now for we must see to many details today. Lord Darby has decided we are to leave for London four weeks hence." ·

Greydon emptied his glass of port and studied the squire's brooding features. "That was a huge dog by ordinary standards we bagged today. I am happy we were able to get him before my departure. Your sheep should be safe now."

"Ummmm," Geoffrey answered vaguely.

"Did it have six or eight legs?" Greydon asked, continuing to stare.

"Eight, I suppose," Geoffrey shook himself and looked at his friend. "What was it you asked?"

"How many legs the wild dog had," Greydon returned with a smile. "Rather unusual beast to have eight, wouldn't you say?"

"I'm afraid I wasn't paying attention. Would you care for more port?" he asked, setting his empty glass upon the table between them.

"Yes." The earl held out his glass and the squire replenished both. "You have been . . . preoccupied these last three weeks, Geoff. I know I am—have not been," he corrected himself, "the best of guests . . ."

"Nothing to do with you, Roland. I've enjoyed your stay. Sorry to see it end."

"You aren't still anxious about Miss Aderly, are you?" he quietly probed.

"Odd—you never were one for names," Geoffrey remarked casually, shifting in his chair. "Audacia has been in my thoughts. That Darby fellow . . . well, I'm concerned." He ended with a shrug.

"Must admit I'm surprised Miss Aderly hasn't returned home. Oh, not because of young Darby. I really didn't think Lord and Lady Darby would welcome a guest in their, er, straitened circumstances." Greydon sipped his port while he watched the other. "If you wished, I could stop in at Worcester on my way to London," he remarked indifferently.

"Unless London is recently moved—or Worcester—it is hardly convenient for you, Roland," Webster returned.

"I merely offer as a friend. I dislike knowing you are upset about the matter. It would be easy enough for me to see how Miss Aderly fares and then send word to you. Save me a night in an inn, in fact. But if you think it unwise . . ."

Geoffrey scrutinized his friend closely. They had not discussed Audacia since the day he had called upon her. "Roland, it would be a great favor if you would stop at Darby Hall," he said slowly. "A great favor."

"It is only for your sake I offer to do so," Greydon put in quickly—too quickly.

A smile grew upon Geoffrey's features at Greydon's serious assurance. Mayhaps it will prove to be a greater favor to yourself, my lord, the squire thought and nodded to his friend.

CHAPTER X

"Audee, Audee!" Helene Darby came running into Audacia's room, grabbed hold of her hands, and whirled her in a circle. "Mother has consented. I am to go shopping with you." She hugged the other close. "I am so happy you came to stay with us, Audee."

"Calm yourself, Helene," Audacia said and laughed. "You will tire yourself before we leave the house."

"Isn't everything wonderful. I can scarcely believe it. Here I have been given the room next to yours and will be allowed to go with you about London." She sighed happily. "Mother says the rooms are too small here, but I think the house is beautiful."

"My chambers at Bedworth are much this size," Audacia answered, looking about the room she had been given upon their arrival at the Mount Street address in Mayfair two days past. "I think this shall suit very well."

"Oh, we shall have such fun. You promised to take me

97

to Madame Tussaud's and the cathedral," the young girl warned.

"I haven't forgotten. Remember I have never seen them either. Your mother will surely consent now that Miss Bea has said she will go with us. I do wish Geoff—Squire Webster was here. 'An escort is so much more proper,' " Audacia mimicked Lady Darby and Helene broke into giggles.

"Do you miss him, the squire, I mean. Is he your beau?" Helene asked, stretching out upon the bed and watching Audacia put her black mane into a neat bun.

"My beau? Goodness, no. Whatever put such a silly thought into your head?" The other laughed.

"You do speak of him oft."

"As I do my father."

"Well, yes. But it would be so exciting to have a beau. Are you certain he is not?"

Audacia rose and straightened her skirt. The high-waisted lilac batiste gown with deeper lavender pinstripes and puffed sleeves showed her coloring and form to perfection.

Despite all of Lady Darby's irritating foibles, she had shown herself an excellent guide in the selection of Audacia's wardrobe. This morning they were to journey to St. James and Bond streets to find the last of the frippery needed to set off the gowns and daydresses that had been made in Malvern. Also on the agenda was a stop at the establishment of Madame Fraiche, a French modiste of some repute. Lady Darby had insisted their ball gowns come from this woman's shop, as her reputation and choice of materials were not to be surpassed. While all this shopping held little pleasure for Audacia, she found she did enjoy the look of her new attire and felt a new confidence.

Examining her form in the looking glass, she wondered how surprised her neighbors at Bedworth would be if they could but see her. And the earl of Greydon, came the unbidden thought. What would he think?

"Audee, you aren't listening," Helene's voice intruded. "When shall you be finished?"

"Right now. Let us go down. You know your mother does not like to be kept waiting."

"Just as I was saying," Helene said, tumbling from the bed. Audacia halted her and motioned for her to straighten her gown while she retied the hair ribbons and smoothed a few stray curls for the young girl. "Mother said my brother Patrick would be coming to London soon," she noted absently.

"Oh? That should please you," Audacia said patting the last curl into place. "I know I would be very pleased to see my brother."

"Patrick and I are not well acquainted," Helene shrugged, "but even were he not one and ten years older than I, I think I should still dislike him."

"That is unkind, Helene. Mayhaps you could come to learn more of him and thus think better of him while he is here."

"Would you help me do that, Audee?" she asked eagerly.

"Of course. Now come along. Mustn't spoil the good impression we've wrought thus far," Audacia said, taking Helene's hand and leading the way.

"It is very strange how Mother lets you speak your mind, Audee. And how she finds ways to approve your behavior. More than once I have thought you were to get a good scold only to hear Mother say little, or nothing," the young girl commented.

"It is only because I am the daughter of a dear friend. Father says our mothers were very close," Audacia answered, but admitted the thought had occurred to her.

"No matter what the reason, I am happier for it." Helene glanced all around as they paused at the top of the stairs. "Do you think we shall be able to find any excitement here?"

"There should be little trouble with that—but be careful of your pranks. I was hard pressed to keep a straight face when Trotter unveiled the bird's nest at supper last eve. Whatever did you do with the pheasant we were supposed to eat?"

"Did you see the look on his face when . . ." Helene fell silent as Miss Bea came to the foot of the stairs. "Good morn, Miss Strowne," she greeted the abigail.

"Lady Darby awaits you both in the salon, Miss Audacia. You had best hurry."

"We were just going there."

"Mayhaps I should come with you today," the abigail said worriedly.

"What trouble could I have with Lady Darby's guiding presence?" Audacia answered. "I promise to be on my best behavior. We are only going for gewgaws and to select the material for our ball gowns."

"Yes, miss," she sighed.

"Why, Miss Bea, are you displeased? Has Trotter . . . ?"

"No, nothing of the sort. I must be fatigued from all the excitement of the journey and getting settled in here. And

100

I can't help worrying about Mr. Ballin . . . and Sir Aderly," she added hurriedly.

"Father's last letter was very cheerful," Audacia assured her.

"More to be worried about. Never knew a happy man who had no problems," Miss Bea clucked.

"Now you are worrying overmuch. Try to rest this morn. I have taken care of all I shall need this eve."

The abigail nodded and proceeded up the stairs. Audacia watched her for a few moments, pondering the change she had noticed in Miss Bea the last few weeks.

"Helene, Audacia—hurry along now. The groom does not like to keep the beasts standing overlong," Lady Darby called entering the hall. She accepted the light pelisse Trotter held for her and waited impatiently while he assisted Helene and Audacia into theirs, then held the door for them.

"There is so much to do," Lady Darby twittered as they settled in the coach, "and I do want you looking your best when Patrick arrives. He is coming very soon." She flashed a toothy smile at Audacia. "Won't he be surprised to see how beautiful you have become? I just know you two will get along frightfully well—just as you did when you were small. I do hope he arrives before our soiree."

Nodding pleasantly, Audacia held a chuckle within. I do not think you truly wish us to be as we were when small, she thought reaching into her memories of Patrick as a little tyrant. Audacia thought of the suit of armor at Darby Hall. How would he look in it, she wondered, then shook away the mental vision of the powerfully built, dark earl of Greydon that came instantly to mind.

* * *

A smart, freshly painted white and black phaeton halted before the stately house at No. 17 Berkeley. The tiger leaped down from his perch and was instantly at the heads of the matched whites drawing it.

"Keep them walking," the Earl of Greydon instructed before striding up the steps and through the waiting open door. His steps hardly faltered as the butler caught the caped coat he shucked from his shoulders and the hat and gloves he tossed.

"Roland, dear boy, when did you return? We had given up seeing you," the Marchioness of Mandel greeted her son as she tilted her head to receive his kiss.

"I have been in London but a night, Mother. You are looking well. And Father?"

"About as usual, sad to leave the country but eager to enter the fray, as always. How have you fared, Roland?" she asked, her sharp dark eyes running over her handsome son.

"Well, as you can readily see." He gave a wry laugh, sitting next to her on the velvet Chippendale settee. "Growing fat and lazy with country ways. Geoff is the flawless country gentleman. You wouldn't believe it if you saw him, Mother. His recovery is more complete than anyone could have hoped. It is as if he managed to forget . . ." The thought remained unfinished.

"He is a fortunate man, then. But you, Roland?" she inquired a second time, her mother's eyes still seeing the unsettled, strained look that had concerned her since his return from Waterloo.

"Do not fret so, Mother." He smiled gently. "I am hale and able. Now, tell me. What have you been busy with? Have the balls and soirees begun?"

"What? Has Geoffrey managed the impossible?" she asked with a laughing glint. "I thought such events were totally *méprisable* to you."

"All men change, Mother," Greydon said with a wink. "After the solitude of Warwickshire, I am hungering for *le multitude.*"

Arched brows greeted his words and the marchioness placed a hand upon her son's forehead. "A fever could be the *only* reason for those words," she told her usually solitary son. Withdrawing her hand, she studied him closely. "Actually it is rather early in the season for a full-fledged round of balls," she told him. "We do have a card for Lord Saltouns' affair, and Monson is having a gala. But these are both to take place in a fortnight."

A trace of disappointment crossed Greydon's features, and he leaned languidly against the back of the settee, pondering what step to take next. He had told himself repeatedly on his hurried ride to London that the disappointment he felt at finding the Darbys already departed was caused by his failure to be able to reassure Geoffrey. But it was Miss Aderly's image, not his friend's, that lingered. Having written the squire of the Darbys' departure, Greydon persuaded himself it was his duty to Geoffrey to pursue the matter.

". . . the oddest thing," the marchioness concluded, "a bid came from the Darbys. Now they haven't been able to be active during the season for several years. Of course, we shall not attend. I cannot imagine Lady Darby's thinking in having something so ghastly early in the season. No one will be prepared to go. But then . . ."

"Did you say Darby? Are they in town?" Greydon asked, his attention all hers.

"What possible interest could you have in the Darbys? I didn't know you were acquainted with them," she noted, surprised by the intensity of his gaze.

"Encountered the son once. Did you say you had a card for a soiree being given by them?"

"It couldn't be called a soiree being so early, but yes," she concluded, seeing his impatience. "As I said, however, we shall not go."

"Mother, if I would escort you, would you consider going?"

"But this family has been in straits for years. They simply aren't part of the ton. They are certain to have a meager draw."

"I haven't known the Greydons were so pretentious," he noted slowly. When she bristled, he took her hand. "They would not have a poor showing if you made it known you would be there. It would not be difficult for you, for one of your beauty and skill."

"What is that brother of mine trying to persuade you to do, Mother?" Lady Lucille Greydon asked, laughing as she entered the salon, her fair coloring and light brown hair as opposite her brother's dark looks as her almost diminuitive form was to his stature.

"My lady," Greydon rose and bowed. "You are in excellent looks." He warmly approved the dancing light in her usually somber gaze. "Your greeting is sincere as always," he smiled broadly.

Accepting his words with a sisterly smile, she laughed once more and brushed his cheek with a kiss before looking to her mother. "What is this rogue trying to fob off this time?"

"He simply wishes to escort us."

104

"My, I fear my ears do misguide me," Lady Lucille said, feigning shock, "for I do believe you said his lordship has offered to escort us, Mother." She took a seat opposite them with easy grace and stared at her brother with mischievous expectancy.

"You are not too old for a brotherly spanking," Greydon quipped brusquely.

"Roland wishes to take us to the Darbys," the marchioness explained. "Do you think we should accept?"

"Darbys? But isn't that the same family whose son . . . ?"

"Lucille, young ladies do not know of such things. Certainly they do not speak of them," her mother reprimanded. Turning to her son, she asked, "Why would you have us go?"

Glancing with concern to his sister, he answered slowly, "It is for Geoff. He asked me to, well, to see that . . . It is very simple," Greydon began again, trying to find words to explain.

"One would not think that from your manner," Lady Lucille teased lightly. "Would it involve a young lady?"

"Yes, and Geoff wants her to be accepted by the ton," he answered quickly.

Surprise and dismay flickered over Lucille's face as she lowered her eyes.

The marchioness eyed her with concern and asked, "This young lady is a member of the Darby family?"

"No." Greydon rose, suddenly irritated by this questioning and distressed by his sister's pale looks. "Miss Aderly is the daughter of a baronet, Sir Maurice Aderly of Bedworth. They are neighbors of Geoff, and it seems he thinks rather highly of Miss Aderly and wishes her to enjoy her visit to London."

"Surely she can do this without our approval?" Lady Mandel commented.

"Mother, it is little enough to do," Lucille said slowly, raising her eyes to meet Greydon's, "if Roland feels we should."

He nodded.

"Then we shall. Roland, you may call on us Thursday next," his mother told him.

"Good. Now, Lucille, fetch your pelisse and bonnet and I shall show you my new whites. They are splendid beasts," he urged her.

"Go along," the marchioness prodded. "You have not been out since our arrival."

"I will just be a moment," Lucille responded after hesitating. "It is good to see you," she said laying a hand on her brother's arm as she passed him.

He bowed slightly and waited until she had left the salon. "Does she still hold a *tendre* for Geoff? Do you know what occurred between them?" he asked his mother.

"She has never spoken of it, but her tears were frequent those first months. I have never understood it, for I was certain they cared for each other. What of this Miss Aderly?"

"I am not sure how Geoff feels toward her. He claims she is merely a good friend and he did ask of Lucille—if she ever spoke of him. If only he would come to London," he ended, pacing away.

"Affairs of the heart are best not meddled with," Lady Mandel warned. "Those who would play Cupid are more oft burned by the shaft than those they would pierce.

106

What is meant to be, will be," she sighed sadly. "What do you think of Miss Aderly?"

Slight color came to Greydon's face at the unexpected question. "I have not . . . met her," he said, turning from his mother's curious gaze. "But Geoff speaks well of her." The earl forced the vision of Audacia from his mind. "Ah, you have returned," he greeted his sister with relief and hurriedly bade farewell to his mother.

CHAPTER XI

The bright April sunshine was held at bay by the heavy damask draperies in Lord Greydon's bachelor quarters bedchamber. A soiree given by Harriet Wilson's fair set had kept his lordship out until early dawn, and he had given orders not to be awakened until late afternoon. His only commitment for the day was the evening escort of Lady Mandel and his sister to the Darbys.

Arguing voices reached Greydon's ears beneath the down pillow, and he reached blindly to pull a second atop it. When the tones faded, he relaxed and stretched his full length, determined to sleep once more. The sound of his door latch and heavy footsteps into his room roused the earl once more. At the squeak of the curtain rings being pulled back, he threw pillows and blankets aside. The brilliant sunlight caused him to blink and shade his eyes while an oath informed the visitor of Greydon's feelings at being so abruptly awakened.

"What? No 'thank you' for not using the trumpet as I oft did in our military days?" Squire Webster asked him plaintively, pouring a glass half full of port and handing it to his friend, who sat on the side of the bed holding his head. "Drink this," he instructed. "Your looks indicate need of it." Taking the emptied glass, the squire returned it to the table and then tossed Greydon his dressing gown.

"When did you arrive in London?" the earl asked as he shrugged into it. "Why didn't you send word you were coming?"

"Only decided a few days past that I was coming," the other returned. "Will you have space in these quarters for me?"

"It will be arranged of course." Greydon, his eyes finally consenting to stay open and his mind shifting into motion, studied his friend. "My God, Geoff!" he exclaimed at the rough-bearded, mud-spattered, worn figure before him. "Are you well?"

Geoffrey waved aside his concern.

"How did you manage to get past Cranby in your state?"

"There are few men with my looks seeking entry into an earl's bedchamber," Geoffrey replied motioning to his empty sleeve. "It does have its uses, you see," he joked.

Greydon's eyes narrowed; his lips tightened; guilt was wrenching him.

"What have you learned about Audacia?" the squire asked as he plopped tiredly into an overstuffed chair. The questions that had driven him in such haste to London would not let themselves be voiced.

"Is the chit the reason for your madcap riding across

England? I assured you I would see to her. Don't you realize you could have . . ."

"Could have done what, Roland? Why am I less fit for the ride than you?" he challenged softly.

"I did not mean that." Greydon waved his hand irritably, hesitant to continue.

"Perhaps it would be best if I stayed elsewhere—my brother may have returned to town by this time," Geoffrey said, rising.

"No, friend. I am sorry—for both my words and my temper. Neither of us is fit for humanity at the moment. Have Cranby see to your needs and rest for a time. Miss Aderly is quite safe. In fact I am to attend a soiree in her honor this eve. The Darbys are opening the season for us. And young Darby has been seen nowhere," Greydon answered the question on Webster's lips.

"I am frightfully worn," Geoffrey admitted. "I should have gotten lodgings and refreshed myself before calling upon you."

"Nonsense, old man. Glad to have you. Told you to come to London. We've had some bloody good times here and will do so again."

"We've both changed since then, Roland," the other returned sadly. "Has . . . have Lord and Lady Mandel arrived?"

"They must have been the first to return. You know my father—eager to see he is not outmaneuvered."

"And Lady Lucille?"

"She came with them, of course. You shall see her this eve. She's in high looks if I may tender a brotherly opinion," Greydon answered.

"I am certain that is true." The squire turned toward

the door. "Excuse me now while I take your offer. When must you leave this eve?"

"Oh, no. You are going to go with me or I shall remain here also. The thought of encountering Miss Aderly alone is not comforting," he half joked. "Sleep till six; we shall still be able to man the parapets in time."

"A letter, sir. From Miss Audacia I believe," Ballin said, handing the missive to Sir Aderly.

The large, gray-haired baronet broke the seal and read hurriedly. "The date, Ballin, what is today's date?

"Thursday, sir. The fourteenth."

"Then it shall be decided this eve."

"May I ask what shall be, sir?"

"Mayhaps the entire outcome of my daughter's time in London. I needn't mince words with you Ballin. The Darbys are holding a soiree for Audacia this eve and who attends shall determine a great deal. Audacia has made no mention of making or receiving any morning calls since their arrival. Only writes of shopping expeditions and strolls in the parks. It may prove that I was very unwise to send her off alone."

"But Miss Strowne is with her," Ballin protested.

"Her aid to Audacia can only be of a limited sort. If the gentry and peers will not accept Audacia, no one can help her," Sir Aderly said shaking his head.

"Shall we join them, then, sir?" the butler asked, restraining his eagerness.

"We cannot. Our work must be completed. If all goes well, perhaps we can carry the letters of patent to London in May."

"Well, then, sir, why are we loitering about?" Ballin asked, striding towards the workshop.

Sir Aderly gaped in surprise. Although a good assistant, Ballin had never before shown anything but restrained interest in the work.

"Is this necessary," Geoffrey protested as Greydon made a fourth attempt at tying the squire's cravat. "I thought you said this was to be a soiree—not a grand ball."

"First impressions are the most important. Do you want the guests to think we are merely deigning to appear on a whim? No, you've been gone from London too long if you have forgotten the importance of dress," his lordship answered, his face contorted in concentration. "Surely you remember Brummel's example?"

"Where did you manage to find these dress clothes in so short a time?"

"Hold steady now. You are worse than a schoolboy and your memory just as faulty. As I explained earlier, Weston aided me. There." He straightened the last fold. "A masterpiece."

Geoffrey turned to the looking glass and was not unsatisfied. As a gentleman farmer he paid heed to little other than comfort in his garments, but this eve he presented a far different aspect. He eyed the effect of the silver blue cravat lying in artistic folds in the lace of the frilled dress shirt and the darker blue of his waistcoat contrasting sharply with the white, snug-fitting breeches and nodded approval.

After shrugging into his own black evening coat, Greydon held out a blue jay-colored coat for Geoffrey.

112

"Are you not rather somber, Roland?" Geoffrey asked, taking in the black breeches, waistcoat, and coat of the other. The stark white of the plain tucked shirt was in complete contrast to the earl's cravat.

"Suits my humor," Greydon said, wondering if he was wise not to tell Geoff they were to escort his mother and sister. What if I err? Uneasy shadows filled his gaze.

"Mine also." The squire thought of the expected encounter at the soiree. What shall I see in her eyes? he silently questioned. "Don't forget to pin the sleeve." His jaw tightened.

Greydon flinched at the look. He motioned Cranby to see to it.

Inwardly sighing, the squire looked past the valet at his reflection. What chance was there?

Seeing his friend's deep frown, Greydon took him by the arm. "We shall be late if we tarry longer." He drew him forward.

A short while later Geoffrey looked out the window of the earl's closed coach as it slowed. "Why this is Berkeley Square." He recognized Landsdowne House. "What . . . ?" He had a sudden insight into Greydon's tenseness as the coach halted before the Mandels' town house.

"Promised to escort Mother and Lucille," the earl said with strained cheerfulness. "Your coming happily evens out the number." He stepped down.

"But I cannot come without warning." The earl's haunted gaze halted his words.

"I sent a note, Geoff. You are expected and welcome."
Taking a deep breath, the squire joined him.

" 'Twill be better here than amongst a crush of strangers," Greydon attempted to explain. "And if you appear as friends less note will be taken of the past."

"Best be to this quickly then." Webster walked past him and through the door held open by an alert footman.

"Earl Greydon. The Honorable Geoffrey Webster," the butler announced to the two women in the salon.

"Geoffrey, it is a pleasure to see you once again," Lady Mandel rose immediately, walking to him with a warm smile.

"And you also." He bowed, his stiffness lessening beneath the sincerity of her greeting. His eyes swung involuntarily to Lady Lucille. Greydon, Lady Mandel, all he cast from his mind. He walked slowly forward and took the hand she offered, raising it to his lips as he hungrily drank in a vision he had despaired of seeing again. He loved her still.

"I was . . . I was surprised that you . . . that is," Lady Lucille faltered, her carefully practised welcome a shambles. She paled, lowering her eyes from his questioning gaze, not daring to reveal further his effect on her.

"I am in London to see a friend, Miss Audacia Aderly," Geoffrey spoke with forced nonchalance. "I imposed on Roland for quarters while I'm in town. He felt obliged to bring me this eve. I am sorry that it dismays you, Lady Greydon," he apologized with a stiff bow.

"Nonsense." Lady Mandel rescued the pair from further damage. "You will always be welcome." She looked pointedly at her daughter.

"Yes, I did not mean otherwise." Lady Lucille managed a smile. "It is good to see you looking so well."

"I am far better than when we last met," the squire agreed.

The smile froze on her lips; her eyes darkened with an old sorrow as she took in the pinned sleeve for the first time. "I do believe we should be going." Lucille turned to her brother, reaching for his arm.

"Our wraps," Lady Mandel said as she nodded to the butler. "It is still cool of an evening," she chatted with Geoffrey. "Ah, here they are."

Greydon took his sister's wrap, laying the tassled silk garment about her shoulders.

Realizing the squire could not do likewise, the butler hesitated momentarily, then placed Lady Mandel's for him.

The earl's jaw clenched as he watched the look exchanged by Lucille and Geoffrey. Had he done no more than bring them pain once again?

For Audacia the day had been filled with the harried activity of last-minute details for the soiree. Accustomed to the small gatherings of the gentry at Bedworth, she could see no reason for Lady Darby's excessive nervousness and went calmly about arranging flowers and checking the various appointments while the other fluttered about. At last the viscountess deemed preparations complete and sentenced everyone to their rooms for rest.

At six the alarm was raised throughout the house as Lady Darby ordered everyone to begin dressing for the evening. Curling irons, petticoats, cravats, and hair ribbons were the cause of much running about as abigails and maids attempted to satisfy all. In her room Audacia found it difficult to restrain her laughter as even Lord Darby's man was seen scurrying back and forth with freshly ironed shirts and unmentionables. Having allowed Miss Bea to

115

assist her with petticoat and gown, Audacia had sent her to aid Helene, who was to be allowed to attend the gathering.

Impatient because of what she considered a long confinement to her room, Audacia decided she would walk about the house. The excitement generated by the others was proving contagious. At the stairs she encountered Trotter.

"Miss, I was just bringing this to you. A boy brought it with instructions it be given you," he said, holding out a white box.

"What can it be?" she asked, looking suspiciously at the box—thoughts of Helene's pranks keenly in mind.

"One will have to open it. Perhaps the sender has enclosed a card," Trotter suggested.

"Please open it for me, Mr. Trotter," Audacia instructed, stepping back.

The impenetrable face didn't flinch even though the gloved hand hesitated before removing the lid. A faint smile came to his lips as he gazed into the box.

Audacia stepped closer and looked also. A soft "ohh" came from her as she reached in and gently removed the posy of wild Warwickshire flowers.

Wood sorrel, greater stitchwort, and white dead nettles, each with its delicate white blossom, combined to make a bewitching fairy's bouquet. All the loneliness Audacia had been carrying within for the countryside was answered by these flowers' delicate fragrance, and her eyes flew eagerly back to the box to see who had met her heart's need. "There is no card," she said, her disappointment keenly felt. "The boy made no mention of who had given it to him? Are you certain it was for me?"

"He said it was for Miss Aderly but did not mention any other name, miss. It is a most unusual posy and must have been meant for you," Trotter offered, bending his usual nonchalance slightly.

"Audacia, why are you standing about there. You should be resting." Lady Darby's voice came from her room's doorway. "What is that you hold?" she asked, stepping briskly toward the pair.

Bowing, the butler withdrew to retake his post at the main entrance. The time for the guests' arrival was drawing near.

"Why, is it a posy of flowers? Oh." The viscountess stared at the bouquet. "You did not tell me you had a beau," she stated accusingly.

"But I have none. Who could have sent them?"

"They are most curious—almost like . . . weeds."

"Some may consider them just that," Audacia noted, keeping a rein on her temper. "But to me they are lovelier than any common rose, for they speak of home to me." She tenderly caressed the fragile foliage.

"Of your home? Oh, then your father would have sent them. Of course, you wrote and told him of our little fete." The viscountess's look and manner eased. "They are absolutely perfect for your gown. Why, look how they reflect the silver tissue. Let me fasten it for you. Patrick will simply not believe his good fortune," she twittered on. "There—lovely, my dear. I must write and congratulate your father on his taste." Lady Darby gathered her skirts in hand. "Helene! Everyone! Come along," she called out and sailed regally down the stairs.

Following slowly, Audacia gazed at the dainty posy and

wondered who had sent it, for her father could scarcely have gotten her letter telling of the soiree. He never would have had time to send the wildflowers. Who?

"My lord," Lady Darby whispered to her husband, "can you believe our good fortune? Why we shall be able to say we had a true crush. Even Lord and Lady Saltoun are here, and you know they attend only the best affairs." She paused as another couple was announced and approached the receiving line.

Busy greeting these newcomers, Audacia did not hear those who were announced next. It was Lady Darby's voice droning another introduction that caught her attention.

"Lady Mandel, may I introduce the daughter of Sir Maurice Aderly, Audacia. Audacia, this is the Marchioness of Mandel and her daughter, Lady Lucille." Lady Darby preened herself through the introduction of yet another much sought-after guest. Greetings were barely finished with this pair when Audacia found her hand engulfed by a much larger one.

"The Honorable Miss Audacia Aderly, I present Lord Greydon. Lord Greydon," the viscountess's voice rolled unctuously on.

Having been benumbed by all the constantly changing names and faces, the name Greydon made no impression. She curtsied and mechanically raised her eyes only when the gentleman's large hand did not free her own.

A sharp indrawn breath marked her recognition of those dark, probing eyes. Pulling her hand back, she found it remained a prisoner.

"My lady," Greydon spoke to Lady Darby while keep-ing his grip, "may I have the honor of the first dance with your guest of honor?"

"Oh, my. I had hoped Patrick would be here," she twittered. "He was to have been Audacia's partner in the opening set. It would be so nice a touch that he and Audacia follow us . . ." The viscountess paused to reflect: her son was tardy and it would be quite a social feather to have this most eligible lord escort Audacia. The gri-mace she saw settle upon the young woman's face as the earl gazed upon her settled Lady Darby's hesitancy. "Of course, my lord. Audacia will be most honored if you would escort her. We shall form the set in just a few moments."

Greydon bowed to Lady Darby and raised Audacia's hand to his lips. His expression remained unchanged as color flared to her cheeks and her foot casually stepped forward upon his highly polished silver-buckled shoe when she curtsied in response.

The impish smile Audacia gave the earl turned to one of pure pleasure when her hand was taken by a gentleman approaching from behind him. "Geoffrey!" escaped from her and she was barely able to restrain the hug she would have given him but for the viscountess's startled "Audacia!"

"Squire Webster is a neighbor from Bedworth," she offered in explanation, squeezing his hand in welcome.

A disapproving frown remained upon Lady Darby's features. "You are quite welcome it seems," she snipped. "My lord." she held Audacia's hand out to Greydon. "It is time to take our places."

Geoffrey winked and smiled warmly at Audacia before the earl led the reluctant miss to the center of the dancing salon.

A murmur ran through those standing about as the two took their place. Greydon, large-shouldered, slim-hipped and raven-haired, was stunningly handsome in his black and white form-fitting evening clothes. Audacia was strangely matched to him in her high-waisted gown of black silk with its overdress of silver tissue. The gown's color was a startling choice for a young miss, but totally effective with Audacia's slim looks and crowning sable locks, which were pulled back and allowed to cascade to her neck's edge.

The two stood intent upon each other alone as they waited for the music to begin. Slowly but surely Audacia felt as if she were being drawn to the earl, that her spirit was awakening and being asked to answer some need. She knew not how she managed to follow the steps but suddenly the last soft notes were fading away and she sank into a curtsy at Greydon's bow.

"Who is that pair?" Patrick Darby demanded of Trotter. The viscount's son had entered the salon just as the dance had begun and like all those there had watched the entrancing couple flow smoothly through the motions of the dance.

"The young lady is the guest of honor this eve—Miss Audacia Aderly. The gentleman is, I believe, the earl of Greydon," the butler answered tonelessly.

"Mother's guest you say. Hmmmm." He eyed Audacia's form appraisingly. "I like not the way the man stares at her," young Darby bit out, shifting his attention to

Greydon. "Mayhaps I shall teach him to treat our guest with proper manners. If this chit is who Mother wrote of, I am, for once, in wholehearted agreement with her plans."

CHAPTER XII

Lady Darby guided Audacia away from Lord Greydon before either of them could speak. "Patrick has arrived. He shall lead you in the next set. Ah, Patrick," she gushed, dropping Audacia's hand to give her own to the haughty young man before her.

He kissed it dutifully and then took Audacia's. "Is this Miss Aderly, Mother? Your letters have not done her justice." His practiced compliments flowed easily. "It is delightful to meet you at last."

Her experience with Lord Greydon caused Audacia quickly to draw her hand back when Darby bowed. This action displeased him and his thin lips creased and tightened slightly.

"Take your places, my dears," Lady Darby prompted, nudging the pair towards the dancers.

Rejoining Geoffrey and the women, Greydon placed himself where he could easily watch Audacia. His smile tightened when he saw Darby capture Audacia's reluctant hand, but it broadened and a light chuckle escaped as only a few steps into the set with Audacia, Darby tripped. "That is Darby," he answered Geoffrey's questioning nod.

"Your . . . Miss Aderly is very attractive," Lady Lucille noted as she watched Audacia.

"I am somewhat surprised at her transformation," the squire answered, his tone very serious. "At Bedworth Miss Aderly's style was rather more rustic."

"Even mannish," interpolated Greydon.

"You know Miss Aderly, Roland?" Lady Mandel asked, her interest stirred.

"Why, no . . . that is, I had seen Miss Aderly during my stay at Web Manor and Geoff spoke of her quite often so that I felt I knew her well—without ever having met her."

Geoffrey's smile at Greydon's discomfort was misunderstood by Lady Lucille, who murmured, "You think highly of Miss Aderly, do you not, Squire Webster?"

Her use of so formal an address twisted Geoffrey's heart as much as her downcast eyes. "She is to be admired for her ability to help others," he answered honestly. "But there are other women I admire for different reasons," he said attempting to catch her gaze.

A knowing smile, tempered by knowledge and maturity, played upon Lady Mandel's features as she watched the interplay between the three beside her. This Season shall be more lively. *Certe,* more interesting than any for many a year, she thought, following her son's gaze to Miss Aderly. "Lady Darby appears very well pleased with the pair," she noted to no one in particular.

Frowns came to both Greydon and Webster.

"Let us dance, Lucille," Greydon said, taking her hand

and leading her towards the dancers before she could refuse.

"Your daughter is very lovely, Lady Mandel," Geoffrey told the marchioness earnestly.

"Yes, but I fear she has placed herself upon the shelf. At six and twenty she has rebuffed too many suitors to be able to hope any shall offer for her hand," she noted with practiced disinterest.

A tiny spark of hope within Geoffrey's heart kindled into a feeble flame.

The music ended once more and the various couples walked from the floor. The salon was becoming very crowded and there was some inevitable jostling, but young Darby bumped against Lord Greydon with far more force than was necessary. Catching his balance, the earl murmured an apology and led Lady Lucille back to their mother.

"The oaf," Darby told Audacia scornfully. "Thinks a title gives him the right to everything."

Taking in the young man's narrowed eyes as he stared after Greydon, Audacia felt a sudden chill. Animosity seemed to hover over Darby. "You should ask Helene for the next dance," she said, seeking to shake her feeling of dislike.

Darby gave a derisive hoot. "Dance with a schoolgirl? My sister no less? What reason could I have for doing so ludicrous a thing?" he scoffed.

"With so many years between your ages," Audacia began, biting back the reprimand that battled to be free, "Helene feels you care very little for her. Your maturity should tell you that a show of affection on your part would please her greatly."

124

Something in Audacia's look caused Darby to change the words he thought to say. Instead he bowed lowly saying, "To please you I would do anything, Miss Aderly. I go to do as you bid."

Restraining her desire to kick the pompous egotist in the seat of his overly tight breeches, Audacia tapped her foot irritably. She sighed with relief at Helene's look of joy as Patrick led her toward the assembling dancers. Free of Darby and of his mother's grasp for the moment, she made straight for Squire Webster, who was talking with the Greydons and Lady Mandel. After murmuring greetings to the others, she placed her hand on his arm. "I am so glad you could come, Geoffrey. It will make London seem all that you said it was. How does my father do? His work must be occupying him, for I have not heard a word since our arrival here."

"I believe his experiments have been going well. The last time I visited him he said he hoped to be ready for the early harvest," Geoffrey offered, smiling at her heightened color and the fact that her eyes had strayed to Greydon.

"It would be so good to have Father here. He told me Daniel would be coming with a friend from school. A Lord Hillern, I believe, and I am so looking forward to seeing him."

"Is this Daniel the beau who sent you that exquisite posy?" Lady Mandel asked with a warm smile.

"Mayhaps that is who is responsible for it," Audacia said to herself, glancing down at the wildflowers. "It has been a mystery to me, for Father would not think to do it and I could think of no one else who would be so knowing of my love of the woods' flowers. But Daniel? No, my brother is not the sort to do it either," she decided.

"You, Geoffrey," her sparkling eyes swung to him. "It was you, was it not? How am I to thank you?"

"Be assured you owe me none," he protested. " 'Twas not I who sent it, although I wish I had thought of it."

Audacia eyed him doubtfully.

"There you are, Audacia. Patrick and I have been seeking you. Lady Mandel, Lord Greydon, Lady Greydon." The viscountess nodded at each patronizingly.

"We were just admiring Miss Aderly's lovely bouquet," Lady Lucille said, breaking the sudden silence. "I cannot understand anyone not being willing to acknowledge such a delightful, delicate tribute," she added, her gaze on Geoffrey.

"Then I feel obliged to solve the mystery," Lady Darby twittered. "Patrick just told me it was he who sent it."

All eyes flew to young Darby. "I am most gratified that it has pleased you so," he told Audacia, bowing.

"Why . . . yes . . . thank you," she murmured, not truly willing to believe it was he who was responsible.

"For my reward I lay claim to this dance," Darby told her, capturing her hand.

One look at Lady Darby told the young woman she dare not refuse.

"Aren't they a lovely pair," the viscountess commented at the two walked away. "Lady Aderly was such a dear friend, God rest her soul. I just know she would have been so pleased to see her daughter and my son together."

"They are to be betrothed, then?" the marchioness asked.

"Of course there has been no formal announcement but . . ." she turned back to watch the pair, her manner leaving only one conclusion.

Looking to the squire, Lady Lucille bit her lip at his growing scowl. There was no doubt that he had not been pleased by the announcement. A heartfelt sigh escaped her.

"I fear we must be taking our leave soon, Lady Darby," the marchioness told her hostess. "Lord Mandel is expecting us at the Earl of Liverpool's—some official gathering," she explained.

"I understand completely, do not fear. We were delighted you could come," Lady Darby simpered.

"We shall look for you at Almacks, Thursday next, then," Lord Greydon told her as he bowed.

A deeper red tinged the viscountess's rouged cheeks. "I fear . . . I fear that will not be possible. I . . . of course, we could attend, but Audacia has no vouchers and I would not think of leaving the poor girl alone."

"Bring Miss Aderly, I shall obtain the vouchers," Lady Mandel told the viscountess, prodded to speak by a telling nudge from her son. "Lady Castlereagh is a dear friend and will gladly oblige me."

"Why, thank you. I know Audacia will be so pleased. I must tell her at once. So kind of you to have come," Lady Darby nodded at the small group, dropped a light curtsy, and triumphantly joined her husband at the edge of the dancers.

"You are the most graceful dancer I have had the happy occasion to partner," Patrick told a skeptical Audacia, as her eyes busily scanned the gathering for signs of the squire.

"If it is Mother you seek," Darby said, "she is there by Father. Let us join them." Taking hold Audacia's elbow, he pushed their way through the crowd to his parents' side.

Lady Darby beamed at the pair. "My dears, what an attractive couple you present. Audacia, I have the best of news," she twittered. "You are to go to Almacks. Lady Mandel has kindly offered to attain your vouchers! To think, you and Patrick shall be among all the ton." She sighed happily. The end of these past troublesome years is at hand, she thought.

"My congratulations, Mother," Patrick bowed. "You have been successful beyond words. And now I have a surprise for you both." He nodded at his mother and Audacia. "You both shall wish to reward me handsomely for this." Darby smirked knowingly. The brunt of his attention fell on Audacia, who was hard put to keep her expression bland. Young Darby raised his hand as if to direct someone to him. Hesitating to show enthusiasm for anything he might proffer, Audacia kept her eyes upon those close about.

"Am I so unworthy of note?" a well-known voice sounded in her ear.

Whirling about, Audacia forgot all of Lady Darby's hard-taught lessons on decorum. "Daniel!" she shouted joyfully and embraced him warmly.

"Mother, Father, I present the Honorable Mr. Daniel Aderly. Mr. Aderly, my parents, Lord and Lady Darby."

Bowing deeply, Daniel acknowledged their nods. "It is a pleasure to meet you both. Father has spoken highly of you for years. Your present kindness to my sister is beyond my gratitude," he told them, beaming happily. "Will you excuse Audacia and I so that we may join the others for this country set?"

128

"Of course," Lady Darby gushed. "We are all here to enjoy ourselves." When the two had walked away she laid her hand upon her son's arm. "Very well done, my dear boy. You would not have been more effective had I coached you. First the flowers . . . and now her brother. I underestimated you, my son."

CHAPTER XIII

Having begged a reprieve from going with Lady Darby to make a morning call upon the Saltouns, Audacia and Helene were enjoying their free morn alone in the small receiving salon when Trotter announced Squire Webster.

"Oh, Geoffrey, I am so glad you could come. Have you seen Daniel yet? He arrived at the soiree just after you left. When shall we all be together?"

"Slowly," the squire said as he laughed, "you take my breath away. First introduce me to this charming young lady," he turned towards Helene.

"Squire Webster, may I present the Honorable Miss Helene Darby."

"Charmed," Geoffrey said gallantly, taking her hand and kissing it lightly.

Tongue-tied by such attention, Helene could only stare in admiring wonder. Then she noticed Geoffrey's pinned sleeve. "Does the lack of your arm pain you?" she asked with youthful bluntness.

"It has not for sometime," he answered her with a smile. "May I sit with you?"

"Were you very sad about losing it? Did it hurt much?" Helene inquired with macabre if youthful innocence as she moved to make room for the squire.

"At the time I was not in a state of feeling much of anything," Geoffrey noted wryly. "But I do seem to recall it hurt like hell's damnation, if you ladies will excuse the language. As to your other question, I have become accustomed to doing without it."

"But isn't there any time you would give anything to have it back?"

Geoffrey smiled at her childish ignorance and artlessness. "Only when I long to dance with a young lady as lovely as you," he answered lightly.

Helene blushed deeply, his conquest complete. "Well, I for one, don't care if you have only one arm," she stated adamantly.

"Thank you," he nodded and both broke into laughter.

"Why is it you cannot dance?" Audacia inquired, a quizzical look upon her features.

"There are many things you have shown me which could still be done by such as I, Miss Aderly. But, dancing?" he shook his head. "Think. Which hand does the gentleman offer to his lady for the minuet?"

Closing her eyes and wrinkling her nose as she concentrated, Audacia drew a curtsy as one would at the beginning of the dance and then raised her right hand. Assuming the gentleman's stance she bowed and raised her left hand. Wordlessly her eyes went to the sleeve pinned upon Geoffrey's left shoulder.

"You see," he noted softly.

"Now wait," Audacia insisted, not admitting defeat. "There has to be a way."

"We had better flee," the squire told Helene with a wink. "For when Miss Aderly begins to ruminate none is safe."

Giggles came from Helene in answer as she looked from one to the other.

"I am perfectly serious," Audacia told them both as she walked to the sofa where they were sitting and took Geoffrey's hand. She tugged until he stood. "What if we would simply change positions?"

"I doubt that I would be handsome in a ball gown," Geoffrey quipped, looking past Audacia's frown at Helene.

"Be serious, Geoffrey," she ordered, making a face at his jest. "Let us try it. I will give you my left hand. Yes, that is right."

After several minutes Geoffrey halted. "It will never work, Audacia. It is too awkward."

"The minuet is not the only dance," she persisted. "This would be manageable for the country sets. But for the waltz . . ."

"Waltz! Are you mad? I could not begin to do that."

Audacia's eyes narrowed with the challenge. "I thought we had banished words such as *not* and *never* some time ago," she commented half angrily.

"But how?"

"There is a way, I know it. Let's see. You are to put

132

your right arm about my waist—thus," Audacia said taking hold of his hand and placing it on her small waist.

"And what shall you do with your right hand?" Geoffrey scoffed.

"Why would it not work to put it on your shoulder . . . like this? One, two, three. One, two, three," she counted out the steps as they moved through them. "Faster now. Helene, hum for us," Audacia called out merrily.

Gradually the awkwardness left their motions as both gained confidence and soon they were waltzing smoothly about the room.

"You see," Audacia told Geoffrey proudly, "I knew it could be done."

The squire's arm tightened as he pulled Audacia off her feet and whirled her in a circle. "You are a treasure beyond words," he thanked her as they halted at last and he released her.

"We shall show everyone, tomorrow, at Almack's," she returned excitedly.

"But, Audee," Helene interrupted, "won't Mother be terribly upset if you allow . . . I mean, are so . . . close to Squire Webster?"

"Under most circumstances I think you would be quite correct. But you see"—Audacia posed dramatically—"the 'unfortunate' squire has to be given special consideration . . . even pardoned for social improprieties."

"You imp," Geoffrey said with a laugh and shook his head. "You are incorrigible."

"Why thank you, sir. *That* compliment is sincere, at least."

"But Mother says you have to be given approval or

permission . . . something, before you can waltz at Almack's." Helene still frowned.

"Such a minor thing will pose no problem," Audacia told her with a laugh.

"Methinks I tarry here too long." The squire arched an eyebrow at the older of the two schemers. "I came only to inquire if you ladies would care to go for a drive in the park this Sunday."

"Oh, Audee, could we?" Helene implored.

"I shall have to ask Lady Darby's permission, but I do not think she shall refuse. Call upon us in any happenstance," she told him, her eyes twinkling and her color bright from the exertion of the dance.

Geoffrey took leave of Helene and then held Audacia's hand. Bowing formally, he kissed it lightly saying as he released it, "Lord Greydon is correct, you are most beautiful."

Before she could recover enough to reply, he had strode from the room and was gone.

"Do not hurry so," Miss Bea admonished Helene and Audacia as their steps drew them farther and farther from her. "It is most unladylike. Moderation!" She sighed heavily and hurried after the two.

"Go ahead, Helene. I shall wait for Miss Bea," Audacia instructed the young girl, looking back at the abigail. "But not too far ahead, now."

"You should not let Miss Darby scamper about," Miss Strowne scolded when she joined Audacia. "It simply isn't proper for a young lady to do so."

"This is the only exercise we have" the other protested. "What harm can be done as long as we can see her?"

134

"None, I suppose," the abigail answered tiredly.

"Let us rest for a few moments on that bench there." Audacia pointed to one of many in this area of St. James Park. "Helene," she called loudly, "stay nearby."

"Miss Audacia, pleeeeease," Miss Bea protested, her cheeks aflame as others in the park stared at them.

"Would you rather we lose sight of Helene? But come, I do not mean to try you. You look so fatigued." Both women sat and Audacia studied Miss Bea closely. "Are you not feeling well? You look exhausted."

Color surged back to the abigail's face. "I—I have not slept well of late. The noise of the city, perhaps. Also I have been . . . troubled by . . . dreams. Oh, nothing dreadful. It is only that I worry about Bal . . . about Sir Aderly—being alone and all."

"Father has written speaking highly of Mrs. Stoddard. She cannot be doing as well as you did but I'm certain her work is adequate." Audacia laid her hand on the other's. "I do wish you would not be too unhappy while we are here."

Forcing a smile, Miss Bea responded, "Of course, I am not unhappy. Only wiser perhaps. One learns so much when one leaves her . . . home behind."

What strange words, Audacia thought. She was distracted as Helene dashed up to the bench and pointed to the street.

"Isn't that the gentleman who danced with you first on the night of our soiree? The one who was with Squire Webster?" she asked.

With her hand shading her eyes from the afternoon sun, Audacia rose and peered more closely at the nearing landau. "Yes, I believe it is," she answered. "That is Lord

Greydon, but I do not think that is his sister with him. Never mind, he is no concern of ours."

Miss Bea joined the two. "Hrrummph, that is no lady with his lordship," she scoffed. "That's a—well, never mind. It is time we return. Lady Darby will wonder what has kept us."

"Look at her hair, Audee," Helene commented, refusing to be drawn away. "It is like those fashion plates we saw in the *Lady's Magazine.*" She reached to touch the locks that had strayed from her bonnet. "I wonder what I would look like in such a style?"

"That is enough, young lady," Miss Bea exclaimed, grabbing Helene's hand and pulling her along. Visions of shorn locks paraded before her as she thought of both her charges' daring natures.

The landau had drawn near enough for its occupants to be clearly seen. A frown came to Audacia's lips as she saw that the woman with Greydon was flirting outrageously with him, and that he was apparently enjoying it. Just as she was about to turn and follow Miss Bea, Greydon's gaze swept over the park. His look caught hers and for a fleeting second the world stood still for them. Then Greydon tipped his hat and the landau was gone. "Ohhh." Audacia stamped her foot in anger at being caught staring. She ran to catch up with the other two.

On a side path, quite close, a hansom cab halted. After giving his companion a lingering kiss, the young man stepped out and motioned for the driver to move on. Rouged lips blew a kiss from the dainty gloved hand as the cab passed. Giving a regretful shrug, the young man cast about and located his quarry.

"Miss Aderly! Miss Aderly, please wait," Patrick

Darby called out; stepping briskly towards the retreating figures.

"Why it is Patrick," Helene exclaimed as the three halted. "Why would he come to the park? He hates fresh air!"

"He wished to spend some time with you," Audacia told her, hoping this was true. "How kind of you to join us." She smiled her greeting. "I know how busy you must be and think it wonderful," Audacia said and brightened her smile, "for you to take time to walk with Helene. Miss Strowne and I will stroll ahead of you," she ended, taking Miss Bea's arm and stepping forward.

Darby glared at Audacia's back, wondering at having been outmaneuvered. Ungraciously he offered his arm to Helene and followed the fast-stepping pair ahead of them. One would think she dislikes me, he thought.

Glancing back just then, Audacia flashed a bright, approving smile at him.

Confidence resurged. It is only that she thinks I care for Helene, Darby assured himself. Why should she not think I am the perfect brother. He straightened. It is the only conclusion, he decided and turned his charms upon his sister, keeping his voice sufficiently loud to carry to the ladies ahead.

CHAPTER XIV

The late afternoon sun broke free of the clouds and filtered through the haze hanging over London. Its bright rays caused a shower of color about the young pair walking slowly back to Mount Street.

"Look, a shower of hundreds of rainbows," Audacia exclaimed to her brother as they paused at the corner of Berkeley Square.

"It is fortunate that it is only the sun's rays, not rain that is causing them," Daniel told her, looking at her thin sprigged-muslin gown. "Does Father know you go about clad in such costumes? I thought Lady Darby was to select your gowns."

"Why, Daniel, you sound like a stuffy old man," she accused. "Everyone is wearing this style. I have not seen you frown upon any of the ladies we passed this day who were dressed as I."

"But they are not my sister. Oh, Audee, you know what I mean."

"You are being unbelievably priggish, Daniel. What has come over you? I can't believe Mr. Darby's company would have this effect on you. What is it you do when you go about with him?" Audacia asked with more than light interest.

A blush came to Daniel's cheeks. Tugging at his cravat, he sought an adequate but slightly inaccurate reply. "We merely see the sights of London," he shrugged off the question.

"Don't think you can fob me off with the likes of that. St. Paul's Cathedral is not likely to be on the list of Mr. Darby's most interesting attractions, nor Madame Tussaud's Wax Museum. If such places were, then Helene and I could go with you. What establishments do you frequent?"

"Some of the clubs, Boodle's, White's . . ."

"Isn't Boodle's notorious for its gambling? Daniel, you aren't!" Audacia looked at him speechless.

"Everyone does it. Why shouldn't I enjoy myself, also. Zeus only knows when I shall be permitted to come to London again."

"Has Mr. Darby taken you to Waitier's . . . to other gaming hells?"

"That is none of your affair."

"But Daniel, your allowance is very meager. How can you afford it?"

"My misfortune has not been great. Indeed I have come off rather well, Audee. Honestly, it is only a few small ventures. I have not and do not intend to wager high

139

stakes. Do you take me for a green lad?" Daniel tried to reassure his sister.

Relief plainly showed upon Audacia's features but she was still uneasy about the matter. Why would Darby be taking Daniel to such places? Surely he realized their fortunes were not large?

"Let us speak of you," Daniel interrupted her thoughts. "Do you have a *tendre* for Patrick?"

A hoot of laughter escaped but Audacia sobered when she saw her brother's grave expression. "Why, you are serious, are you not?"

"Lady Darby and Patrick seem to think you will be announcing your betrothal at any time."

Audacia bit her lip in frustration, taking his comment for hyperbole. *So, they were obvious to everyone.* "What would prompt the pompous Mr. Darby to consider one as lowly as I?" she asked sarcastically.

"Darby's not pompous. He's a jolly good sort," Daniel disagreed. "And I think he cares for you."

"Cares for me? Little do you know the man. He cares for nothing other than his pleasure," Audacia returned curtly.

"You have only known him a short time. It is not like you to be so harsh in your judgments. Look at how he has gone out of his way to help me and to make your stay here more pleasant."

"The Darby's have done much, I know. That is why I have done no more than try to avoid Patrick. It is so awkward. There is just a feeling I have that they are plotting." She hesitated. Daniel's look of disbelief halted her.

"You are being missish now, like all women," her

brother scoffed. Not heeding the warning in his sister's look, he dared continue, "Women simply must lean on men, be guided by us."

"Daniel," came threateningly as they halted before the Darby's residence.

"After all how can you know what is best for yourself," he went on condescendingly. His words halted when he saw Audacia's glare.

"If you know what is best for you, I suggest you do it," she said cryptically as he backed out of her reach.

"Put that umbrella down, Audee. It wouldn't be at all ladylike. Audee, Lady Darby will see . . ." Daniel's words were left unsaid as he decided a simple retreat was the wiser strategy.

"Men," Audacia said disgustedly, watching her brother dash away. I do wish Father were here, she thought. Perhaps Geoffrey will speak to Daniel. And I must find a way to inform Mr. Darby that I heartily disapprove of his taking Daniel to such places. She hurried inside. It was nearing the hour to begin dressing for the evening at Almacks.

"Patrick is so thoughtful," Lady Darby said for the tenth time as the coach journeyed towards King's Street and Almacks. "What lovely flowers."

The pink-white of the mound of wild pear blossoms against the waxed sheen of their green leaves was the perfect complement for Audacia's gown of true green. Neither too vivid nor too pale, the soft shade of the gown highlighted her healthy glow and raven hair. A deep green satin ribbon gathered the gown slightly beneath her breasts, letting it drape in soft folds that barely concealed her willowy form. A matching ribbon held a simple ivory cameo against her slender neck. Additional wild pear blossoms had been arranged throughout her coiffure by Miss Bea. The freshness and delicateness of the awakening earth, the look and feel of joyful spring had been captured in her appearance this eve.

The viscountess's words passed unheeded; an inner sense told Audacia that Patrick was not the one who had conceived the effect of the blossoms. But who? Someone who knew her wardrobe in detail—knew which gown she would choose. Lady Darby? Audacia mentally shook her head; the viscountess was sincere in her belief that her son was responsible. Lord Darby then? She turned her head to study the nodding shadow of the viscount in the coach's inner gloom. Compassion for him flared. He was far too busy surviving the rigors of his family to think of her, Audacia concluded.

"Remember"—Lady Darby's finger jabbed Audacia's arm—"you are not to waltz until you have been given approval. Consequences will be terribly dire if you would. Also, Patrick has promised to come to Almacks and to bring Daniel. It would only be proper for you to save your first waltz for my dear son," she twittered gaily. "You simply cannot know how fortunate you are."

In the dim light of the coach, Audacia raised an eyebrow skeptically. She did long for a way to end this constant intimation. Her conversation with Daniel had strengthened her dislike of Patrick and raised further suspicions about his character, and she longed for her father's presence.

I will not let them ruin my season, she told herself, as her mind jumped to the scheme planned for Geoffrey this

142

eve. It was daring, she admitted, for the ton could decide the idea "indelicate" and turn up their noses at such audacity on the part of so unimportant a miss. It matters not, she resolved, for it is only a first step. With the confidence Geoffrey gathers from this it should be simple to encourage him to take a wife. This eve I shall watch closely to see what kind of miss interests him and then we shall—

"Here we are," Lady Darby's excited voice intruded. "Remain calm, Audacia. The first impression is the most important. Keep your composure at all times."

It was with great restraint that Audacia held in check the face she wished to make at the footman who barred their entrance.

"But Lady Mandel assured us that there would be no problem," Lady Darby insisted to the man.

After much whispering a page was sent off while the Darby party waited impatiently. After a brief time a tall-ish, haughty woman glanced their way, then fluttered her hand. Immediately the footman stepped aside.

"That was the Countess Levien," the viscountess whispered to Audacia as they entered the main room.

The time was well after nine and already a large group had gathered, for no one was permitted entry after eleven. Lord Darby excused himself at once and made for one of the many card rooms arranged about the outer edges of the ballroom. Lady Darby paused after his departure; coldly indifferent stares from the dowagers who had noticed them dismissed her and Audacia. Encouraged by friendlier glances from the men, she led Audacia towards the still unfilled seats at one side where she had noticed a few ladies who had attended her soiree.

"Why, Lady Darby. I had *no* idea you would come to Almack's," a large woman in a bright red turban said, her inflection making it clear that it was a great surprise that she had been allowed entry.

Disliking her snobbish tone and look, Audacia began, "But if the door is large enough for . . ."

"It is very pleasant to return here," Lady Darby cut her off abruptly, realizing the words to come. "You are looking very well, Lady Firbaine, and your turban is so attractive," she gushed, hoping to draw the woman's attention from Audacia. "Please excuse us, my lady. I see Lady Mandel has arrived and I must thank her for her kindness to my guest." With a falsely bright smile she turned, taking Audacia's hand to make certain she followed. "Never again say the first words that come to you," the viscountess hissed as they walked. "You could have ruined it all."

"But she was insulting . . ."

"The entire world insults everyone and everything. Learn to ignore such remarks. I shall not have all my plans ruined by your careless words." Her tone was low, but the angry threatening sparks in her eyes startled Audacia. "Oh, Lady Mandel. What a great pleasure to see you once again."

Stung by the reprimand and questioning just what plans would have been done away with by her behavior, Audacia stood quietly aside as the two older women exchanged trivialities.

Taking this for shyness, Lady Lucille attempted to make her more comfortable. "Why do we not have some lemonade and find seats," she offered with a smile.

Grateful to be removed from staring eyes, for Audacia

felt everyone was gawking at Lady Darby, she nodded her assent.

"Squire Webster has mentioned you are fond of animals," Lady Lucille continued as they walked. "I recommend you do not attempt to see the menagerie they have at the Tower. The poor animals' treatment should be an embarrassment to all."

"I wish I had not seen them. It is so cruel. Half the beasts are sick and need far more care than was evidenced," Audacia replied, her ire rising at the thought of the mange-ridden lions. "If only there was something that could be done."

"Attempts have been made, without success. Perhaps it is time I speak to Father again."

"Please do," Audacia urged, taking a new assessment of Lord Greydon's sister. "I am so relieved you are not like your brother," she said, forgetting to think before speaking.

"But I thought you had not met my brother before the soiree."

"Of course I had not," Audacia stumbled, her cheeks flaming red. "It is his—his looks. They give him a grim appearance while you are so . . . gentle."

"The war, I think, has done that to Roland. When he first returned after Waterloo we were fearful for him. He was so silent, almost disconsolate. But then the war changed many." A deep sadness swept over Lady Lucille. "So many lost. So much altered," she said lowly. "It is as if Roland broods over—" Catching herself, she paused. "But these matters mean nothing to you" came hurriedly. "Let us speak of your animals."

"What is of such consuming interest?" The firm voice

intruded into the young women's lively chatter a few moments later.

"It would be of little concern to you, Roland," Lady Lucille laughed, looking up at the tall figure before them. "I had thought you were joking about coming." She peered at him quizzically. "Was there not something said about Almack's being far too staid?"

"Geoffrey desired to see the place," he tossed back easily. "And I think I shall leave you in his hands if Miss Aderly will kindly consent to dance with me," Lord Greydon told his sister, his eyes all the while on Audacia.

"Do go, Miss Aderly," Lady Lucille prompted, "the music is delightful and Roland an excellent dancer."

"Yes," Geoffrey added coming from behind Greydon. "I shall entertain Lady Lucille."

Something in the squire's look urged her to go. Stifling the urge to give his lordship a set down, she held out her hand.

Wordless, Greydon led her to the dance floor.

"They present a handsome couple, do they not," the squire commented as Lady Lucille's eyes followed them. The pale cream color of Greydon's evening clothes complemented Audacia's gown. "You are in high looks this evening, also," he dared.

Her eyes refused to meet his. "Thank you," she breathed softly.

Suddenly tongue-tied, Geoffrey could only gaze in questioning wonder, taking in the delicate brown of her coif and recalling that her downcast eyes were much the same color.

"Have you been well?" Lady Lucille asked, raising her

146

eyes to his; her tone, her look attempted to break the stiff, formal politeness of their last encounter.

"I was never one who tended toward illness," he replied. "The only time I was abed was after my arm was ..." The words died as Geoffrey saw Lady Lucille wince and blanch. "How thoughtless of me. I didn't mean to ... there is no reason ..." He fumbled desperately for words, his hope slowly sinking with his heart. "I—I have been quite well," he ended wretchedly.

"I am happy you are fully recovered," she responded, her color slowly returning.

The two sat in silence until Greydon and Audacia rejoined them. The faces of the seated couple showed clearly that something was amiss.

"Geoffrey has been boring you with his dull agricultural experiments, I fear," Lord Greydon noted lightly, attempting to relieve the strained atmosphere.

"They are very important," Audacia protested, defending her friend.

"I would be happy to hear of your work," Lucille noted, quickly looking to Geoffrey with a weak smile.

"Then I shall impart as much as you wish," he offered sincerely.

"Geoffrey, isn't that a waltz they are preparing to play," Audacia asked excitedly, watching the assembling dancers.

"But you must not waltz until you have been given approval, Miss Aderly," Lady Lucille cautioned. "Here is Mother; she can introduce you to the patronesses."

The required formality was completed with amazing ease, after all the fuss about its necessity. Audacia's one thought was to return to Geoffrey when Lady Jersey's waspish voice commanded, "Lord Greydon shall have the honor of your first waltz, Miss Aderly."

"That was unkind," Countess Levien noted to her co-hostess as Audacia walked away with her consigned partner. "That green young miss had another beau in mind. She looked as if she could eat poor Lord Greydon, and he such an *eligible.*"

"Then let us say I have done her a favor," the other returned caustically and dismissed the matter.

On the dance floor Lord Greydon remained impassive to Audacia's glare. "I for one, do not make it a habit to tread upon another's foot," he noted with an ironic half-grin. "You may rest assured you shall remain unscathed."

Audacia's eyes flashed, but her ire quickly subsided as the music began, and as if by magic she was being lightly whirled about the crowded room. Greydon's strength flawlessly guided them through the fluid motions of the beguiling waltz.

Her heart in her throat, Audacia dared to look at him. His eyes captivated hers and the sensation that flowed through her took her breath away. As the last strains sounded and he released his hold, she was reluctant to part from him.

"Not one of your lovely toes has suffered damage," he noted, while his ironic eyes continued to hold hers.

"Really, my lord," Audacia retorted, vexed that he had broken her mood so abruptly. With that she hastened to rejoin Geoffrey and Lady Lucille. It was with relief that she found them chatting amiably for she had noticed the intensity of Geoffrey's eyes as he watched his companion.

For the next half hour she had little time to watch the pair as she wished, for all the gentlemen present wished the pleasure of her hand in dance and she was ever occupied. When at last the next waltz was announced, she laughingly pleaded fatigue and escaped back to the squire. Taking his hand, she urged him to rise.

He held back and shook his head numbly, blushing beneath Lady Lucille's gentle, inquiring look. "I cannot."

"We both know you can."

"But they may never allow you to return here. Even Lord Byron was cut by all here not two weeks past."

"It matters not if that occur. Then I may return to Bedworth the sooner," Audacia tossed his concern aside. "Come."

Her confident, loving smile pleaded her case successfully and Geoffrey followed her with a gulp. Facing the guns of the French army had not tied as many knots in his stomach as this.

Low murmurs and questioning exclamations followed by a deafening hush greeted the new couple's arrival on the dance floor.

"It is too late," Audacia told Geoffrey, reading his thought to escape. "Let us begin slowly," she instructed as the music began.

Rejoining his sister after returning his latest partner to a smiling mother, Lord Greydon watched his waltzing friend in amazement.

"Did you know this was planned?" Lady Lucille asked.

"It is impossible," Greydon said to himself, "but he is doing it."

"This has to be Audacia's doing. I begin to feel she is well named," his sister said with an odd laugh. "Do you know if he loves her?"

The muscles along the earl's jaws flexed as his look of rejoicing clouded.

"Does he?" Lady Lucille asked once more.

"I do not know," he answered after a long pause. "I simply don't know."

His sister gave Greydon a long, thoughtful look, then followed his eyes back to the pair. Other dancers were joining them now. Low huzzas granted approval to the unusual pair as they danced past, their faces full of the excitement and exertion of the moment.

How long since Geoffrey has looked so totally alive, so completely happy, Lady Lucille thought. But that I were the cause of it. If only I had never questioned my love. Looking to her brother, she felt a further pang. The shadowy, brooding look that haunted his eyes had returned.

CHAPTER XV

"Look at this." Helene Darby pushed the latest *La Belle Assemble* magazine beneath Audacia's nose. "I think this would suit me best." A slender finger indicated a coif in the latest French style known as à la Diana. "And this." She leafed pages rapidly. "In this you would be irresistible with your raven hair."

"But there is hardly any hair there," Audacia protested looking at the mode of à la Circe. "It must be but inches long."

"That is what makes it stylish. Don't you ever pay attention? Why don't we cut ours? You could do mine and then . . ."

"Oh, no." Audacia shut the magazine. "If anything, I have grown a little wiser during my stay here. Your mother would be very displeased," she told Helene firmly.

"Now you are beginning to sound like her. What is

151

happening to you? You never want to play anymore," the young girl declared in disgust.

A knock at the door saved Audacia from having to reply.

"Miss Audacia, her ladyship wishes you to come to the receiving salon," Miss Bea told her, opening the door.

"Have you any idea why?" she asked, still awaiting the reproach she had seen on the viscountess's features after her waltz with Geoffrey at Almack's. As far as Audacia was concerned that evening had been triumphant. Not only were they applauded at the end of the music but others had demanded the right to dance with the squire and he was given little rest the remainder of the evening. The only false note was Lady Lucille's reaction, which puzzled Audacia, who had decided Greydon's sister was fond of Geoffrey. That lady had spent the rest of the evening with a tight smile upon her features, watching Geoffrey in dance after dance with the eager young matrons and the more daring of the eligibles. Never once did she approach the squire and he, too overwhelmed with attention, was able to search her out only once. That once, by sad chance, she had already been claimed for the dance and did not see his approach or disappointed mien.

But Lady Darby had been another matter. Thunderclouds had threatened at Audacia's return to her side. Only Lady Jersey's and the other patroness's enthusiastic approval saved her from a tirade.

Patrick's failure to arrive worsened matters, and it was with frigid coldness that the small party climbed into their coach. The viscountess had been cooly polite ever since and all of yesterday, despite several returned morning calls, their first since their arrival in London.

"Young Mr. Darby is with her ladyship, miss," the abigail offered as explanation.

"Then you shall come with me, Helene," Audacia told her young friend.

"But, miss," Miss Bea began to protest.

"I am certain Mr. Darby would wish to see his sister," she cut the abigail off adamantly, taking Helene's hand and walking out.

"Audacia, my dear, here you are. Patrick has called upon us to apologize for not appearing at Almack's and to make it up to you," Lady Darby gushed in greeting. Some of her warmth cooled as she saw Helene behind Audacia. "Have you no lessons?" she asked bluntly.

"I assisted Helene, my lady. All of her work has been completed. And done rather well," Audacia said with a satisfied smile.

"An additional reward should be given you for such good care of my sister," Patrick said, stepping up and laying an arm casually about Helene. "It shall be a ride in the park. Come, my phaeton awaits us." He removed his arm and bowed with a flourish.

"Helene and I would be most pleased to accept your kind offer, Mr. Darby. In truth, it is kind for you to reward your sister so generously," Audacia answered sweetly, giving a small curtsy. "Come, Helene, let us fetch our bonnets and light pelisses."

Frowns followed the two from the salon.

"Can you not handle a simple invitation for a drive?" Lady Darby asked sarcastically.

"I was not responsible for the brat's appearance here.

You heard the way Miss Aderly twisted my words. This courting is . . ."

"Necessary," his mother ended for him. "As the cause of our misfortunes you should appreciate so simple a solution. There shall be no more bungling." She shot him a meaningful glance.

"But they would not admit me. I have explained that. Who wishes the company of the snobs that frequent Almack's anyway," he sneered. "There never was a duller gathering."

"I mean to be among them, and to see you there also," Lady Darby swore.

"Never fear, Mother, you shall," he responded to her vehemence. "If Audacia will not be persuaded by fair means—" Patrick nodded pointedly, his words cut short by sounds of the pair's returning steps.

Elegant phaetons, barouches, and landaus paraded along Rotten Row in the afternoon sunshine. Helene was busy gawking about, taking in all the sights while Audacia was being thankful young Darby's hands were fully occupied by the reins.

Several persons nodded or called out greetings to Audacia as they passed, recalling her daring at Almack's for one of England's brave.

She had begun to think it odd that only the dandyish, the more disreputable looking, greeted Darby for she had supposed he moved in the higher circles of society. More than passing reflection was impossible, however, as Helene peppered off questions about the people, carriages, and even about the naming of the parading area frequented by the ton—Rotten Row.

"I believe it is connected with James the First," Audacia explained somewhat hesitantly, uncertain if her recall was true to fact. "The king and his messengers made their way to Parliament and about their other business matters through this street, and it was then lined with dilapidated buildings and occupied by all manner of beggars and footpads—hence the name."

Darby's team lurched forward suddenly, ending all thoughts of explanations. The number of those driving along Rotten Row had steadily increased until the road was very crowded. Misbehavior by any team was dangerous to its owner and all those close by. Drawing heavily on the reins with a curse, Patrick steadied the team, but not before the wheel of his phaeton locked with that of a passing landau. His oaths at the mishap ended when his eyes encountered the dark, cold eyes of the earl of Greydon.

"Hold them steady," Greydon's cold voice demanded harshly. Skillfully, he backed his matched whites, and the wheels slipped free with no spokes broken on either. "So sorry for the inconvenience, Miss Aderly, Miss Darby," he noted, doffing his hat.

"Those are most magnificent beasts," Helene responded enthusiastically, ignoring Patrick's consternation. "Why, Squire Webster, how nice to see you," she greeted the second gentleman in the earl's landau. "How did it go at Almack's? Audacia is such a tease she would not tell me aught but that you danced," the young girl babbled away at the slightly embarrassed squire.

"It went just as she thought it would," he replied, disengaging an attractive female's hand from his arm and shifting a little from her. The action proved futile as she merely followed.

Audacia suppressed the desire to laugh at Geoffrey's apparent discomfort. Humor left her when she took in Greydon's companion, equally attractive and as daringly clad as the other. This woman stared challengingly at Audacia and wrapped her arm possessively through Greydon's.

The earl's features darkened. "Handle the reins more gently next time," he reprimanded Darby and drove on.

"Oh, I wish he had not gone on," Helene cried, her disappointment plain. "I wished to ask the squire—,"

"You are far too forward, Helene," Patrick scolded her angrily, flicking the reins much more forcefully than was necessary and nearly causing another mishap. "Until you learn better manners you shall not accompany me again."

"But Squire Webster did not object to Helene's inquiries," Audacia threw in, disliking Patrick's tone.

"You've said quite enough," young Darby snapped irritably, tossing a hard-eyed glare at her. After a tension-filled pause, he continued, "Helene is my sister, after all. It is fitting that she take guidance from me—without interference, even from you," Darby concluded pompously.

Audacia murmured polite agreement. Patrick's look frightened her. Her dislike of his mother's constant prattle about betrothal turned to apprehensive dismay.

The quieter noises of night filled the house on Mount Street. For once Lady Darby had no soiree, fête, or ball for them to attend and all were abed early.

Audacia tossed to and fro in her bed, a dream disturbing her sleep. It was as vivid as reality. Helene was cutting and

156

recutting her hair as quickly as it grew back, and the room was filling with mounds of black hair. In the midst of this walked Greydon and Geoffrey, eyeing the discarded curls with jaundiced eyes. Both roared with laughter and then snapped their fingers. Thinly gowned women appeared, their coiffures elegantly à la Diana. They took the men by the arm, leaning provocatively close. Greydon pointed to her. The women stared, then laughed mockingly as they turned back to the earl, raising their lips to receive his kisses.

"Audee! Audee, wake up. You're dreaming," a voice insisted. "Wake up."

Her eyes flew open and Audacia stared wildly to see where the squire and Greydon had gone.

"It is only I," young Helene assured her, holding the candle flame nearer her face. "I could not sleep. May I sit with you for awhile?"

Audacia shook off the last webs of her too vivid dream. Patting the side of her bed, she moved over to make room for Helene to sit. "What is bothering you?" she asked. "Surely you aren't letting your brother's words upset you?"

"I can't help thinking about it, but that is not what truly bothers me. Don't you see how . . . countrified we must look with our long, long hair? Everyone we saw today was wearing it cut short in the current style. Didn't you see how that woman with Lord Greydon stared? I know mother would agree to it if she could see how I looked with mine done à la Diana. Won't you do it for me, Audee? Please? If Mother disapproves I can wear a spinster's cap until it grows back. Please?" she pleaded, her young face woebegone. "I can say I did it, if you wish, but

I know it will not look right if it is my hand that cuts it," Helene ended with impish honesty.

Sitting upright, Audacia reached out and held the young girl's unpinned locks back from her face. Her nose wrinkled in concentration.

"Do not think that hard, Audee," Helene laughed.

"Hush, or you shall wake the house," she returned soberly, "and then I could not cut your hair."

"Oh!" Helene clamped her hands over her mouth but jumped all over the bed in her excitement.

"Stop it before you trample me to death." Audacia laughed, tumbling from the bed. "Let me light this lamp. Now, put the rug beneath the door. Miss Bea might walk the halls. She has not been sleeping well of late. I must see what I can do to cheer her in the morn," she told Helene as she began to go through her sewing box. "Ah, here they are." Snapping the scissors, she ordered, "Bring the lamp to the vanity. Are you certain you wish to do this?"

With a nod Helene sat. "Go on, do it."

Letting out a deep breath, Audacia took hold the first lock of brown, wincing as the scissors sliced through it. "A keepsake?" she asked, holding it over Helene's shoulder and looking at her reflection in the mirror.

"Of course," the young girl quipped. "Don't you know it is quite the thing to send a beau one's lock."

"And you have a beau, miss?" the other returned, attacking the remaining length.

"Not yet, but Miss Bea is always saying it is best to be forearmed. Well"—she held up the shorn lock—"now I shall be."

Joking halted as Audacia continued to work. When she halted it was with a satisfied smile. "In the morn we shall

158

use the curling iron. You shall be a very pretty young lady," she added, not unjustifiably as the short style did become Helene's roundish face.

"Father will like it," the young girl said determinedly, "and perhaps Patrick and Mother as well." Helene rose and brushed the hair clippings from her shoulders. "Thank you, Audee." She hugged her close, tears coming to her eyes. "I am *so* glad you came."

"No tears," Audacia ordered, giving Helene a squeeze before sending her away. "Now off to bed with you. Come straight here when you rise. I'll have Miss Bea ready the curling irons."

"Good sleep, Audee."

She nodded. After Helene was gone she sat before her looking glass. "So . . . shortness is the current *style.*" She twisted and pulled her hair about. "Then shortness is what you shall have." Gritting her teeth, she took hold a handful of hair and cut. "There is no stopping now," she told herself, and the raven locks fell unheeded, soon covering Helene's tawny ones.

Daniel Aderly lurched drunkenly away from the gaming table. Picking up his co-signed marks, Patrick Darby sauntered after him. He signaled the waiter to bring a bottle of port to the table where Daniel had collapsed. "Take a drink," young Darby urged, "it is just the thing you need."

"How much—much have I lost?" Daniel sputtered, raising his head from his arms.

"Not too much, do not fear, I have signed for all your losses," Patrick assured him. "Drink," he prompted once again. "Then we shall move on. A change is all that is needed to alter your luck."

Quaffing the glass of port, Daniel nodded. His bemused brain held no other thought than that he had to recoup his losses.

"I'll bring the port," Darby said, rising and prodding Daniel to stand. "At the next gaming hell your luck will surely change." Motioning for the footman to assist the lad, he followed to the waiting coach, a well-satisfied leer marking his features.

CHAPTER XVI

The last curl was finished for Helene when Lady Darby was heard humming in the hall outside Audacia's bedroom. "Good morn, my dear . . . *eeeek!*" 'Pon my soul, what have you done to yourselves?" she exclaimed, her supremely happy expression transposed into one of utter alarm.

"Miss Bea," Audacia cried out as she ran to catch the swooning viscountess.

"I told you her ladyship would go into hysterics," the abigail scolded as she ran into the room and helped Audacia support Lady Darby. "Come, my lady, lie down for a few moments. I have my vinaigrette right here." She pulled a small bottle of Potter and Moore smelling salts from her apron pocket and handed it to Helene for opening.

One sniff was enough to restore Lady Darby, who sat upright, her discomfiture apparent in her high voice.

"Audacia, what have you done! What am I to do? And Lady Lucille will be here any moment. Oh, dear me. How could you?" she wailed.

"Mother." Helene waved the smelling salts past Lady Darby's nose to get her attention. "What do you think of me?"

"Out of my way, Helene. This is not the time for your childishness. Isn't it enough Audacia has done such an outrageous deed."

"But Mother, look at my hair," the young girl implored, tears threatening.

"Helene does look very charming, doesn't she?" Audacia asked pointedly, putting her arm about the girl's shoulders.

"You have taken part in this nonsense also," Lady Darby exclaimed, seeing at last that Helene's tawny mane was also gone. Her eyes narrowed. "Why . . . I do believe it is an improvement. Yes." She rose from the bed and turned her daughter about, critically inspecting each angle. "It is. You may even be said to be comely," the viscountess told a beaming Helene. "But for you, young lady." Her accusing eyes turned to Audacia. "What *are* we to do?"

"A slight curl about the face would improve it, my lady," Miss Bea cautiously offered.

"Lady Lucille will be coming soon. Is there time to achieve some semblance of looks?"

"What is this about Lady Greydon? I have made no plans with her," Audacia said, interrupting the discussion for which she had no liking.

"Oh, dear, did I forget to mention it? Lady Mandel suggested at Almack's that you and Lady Lucille go on an

162

excursion of the city. Her daughter being familiar with all the popular sights. Well, you had only managed to see the Tower since our arrival and I knew you would be so pleased . . . but now. . . . Surely now you shan't want to go—to be seen?"

"Lady Lucille's hair is only slightly longer than mine," Audacia defended herself with a note of belligerence.

"All the young ladies are wearing their hair like this," Helene said earnestly. "Everyone, look at this," she urged scooping the *La Belle Assemble* magazine from the vanity and holding it out to her mother. The à la Diana etching on the cover was proof of her words.

"Ready the curling irons," Lady Darby ordered as she gazed at the picture. "Perhaps this is not a disaster," she told Audacia in reprimanding tones, "but hurry. I wish you ready when Lady Greydon calls for you." With a shake of her head she forestalled the question on the other's lips. "Do not tarry. The Greydons are an important family. We must not displease them in any way."

"Them," thought Audacia. Is Lord Greydon to come also? Chagrin swooped over her and she reached to touch curls that no longer were.

"It is rewarding to see you show some concern over your actions," Lady Darby noted smugly. "Hurry with those curling irons . . . and not too hot either," the viscountess ordered Miss Bea. Motioning at Helene to follow her, she marched from the room.

The abigail followed, heaving a sigh, and Audacia confronted her looking glass. The reality of day clouded what had been reflected in the night.

* * *

163

"Where did you say my son was staying?" Sir Aderly asked Ballin.

"On Grosvenor," replied the languid valet patiently, "at Lord Hillern's bachelor quarters."

"Yes, that is it. Can't seem to get that boy's name in mind. Well, let us go there first, then. I wish to see how he has fared. Find a hansom. I'll be along directly."

Straightening from his relaxed pose, Ballin drained his ale and hurried from the ale room to the enclosed courtyard of the White Swan. Several coaches were assembled there now, some taking on passengers while others were at the end of their journey. Grooms, harnessed teams, and travelers of all sorts and sizes filled the area with noisy chatter and clatter. Wending through to the street, Ballin was able to hire one of the many waiting cabs and had transferred the baggage by the time Sir Aderly appeared.

"Would ye not prefer to stop by Lord Darby's first?" Ballin asked with overt casualness and inner hope. "It is a wee bit early for a young gentleman on his first visit to London to be roused out," he noted.

"Must be nigh near noon," Sir Aderly returned. "I trust my son has not been cavorting about like any ordinary jackanapes. He's always been steady in his ways."

The housekeeper at the address on Grosvenor would do little more than raise her nose at Ballin and repeat that the young man had not returned as yet. "I've not seen the viscount or that Mr. Aderly for nigh two days. Not uncommon for young bucks," she clucked. "But this is a respectable house. They do their misbehavin' elsewhere," she ended and shut the door in his face.

"Let us arrange for rooms at Pultney's," Sir Maurice

164

ordered when the valet reported Daniel's absence. "Good lad. Knew he'd be about the business of the day. As soon as we are settled in, you can take word of our arrival to Lord Darby and inform him I shall call upon them this eve." He settled his large frame as comfortably as he could in the small hansom. "It will be good to see them both. You were quite right, Ballin. This small interruption of our work shall enable us to attack the problems with renewed vigor when we return home."

While Sir Aderly voiced his satisfaction, Ballin could but question the wisdom of their journey. Now he was becoming convinced that his misgivings were well-founded.

Audacia's hand froze on the knob. The voices on the other side of the receiving salon's doors told of Lord Greydon's presence within. She stamped her foot in annoyance at her sudden hesitation. This is ridiculous. What do you care what the man thinks, she scolded herself lightly under her breath. Your aim is to give the man a set down, came the mental reminder. The sound of Geoffrey's laughter ended her indecision.

The squire was the first to see her. He halted in midword. "My lord," he said dumbly, causing all in the salon to turn their attention to a very uncomfortable Audacia.

"You have joined us at last, my dear," Lady Darby twittered nervously in the ensuing silence.

Greydon bowed, his face impassive under Audacia's challenging glare, while Geoffrey continued to stare.

"Never thought you to be one for these wild ladies' notions of style," he spoke at last, causing her to blush.

"Does become you, rather . . . well." He stumbled for an appropriate end while Audacia's cheeks grew redder.

"We had better be off," Lady Lucille said, seeking to rescue both of them, and rose. "The sun shall become too warm if we tarry too long. I do hope you are not too fatigued from all the Season's exertions," she said to Audacia, "for we have a very full day planned. Squire Webster even arranged to have a picnic packed for us."

"That shall be a most pleasant treat," Audacia answered, giving Lady Lucille a smile of appreciation.

"Roland thought you might enjoy strolling through Kensington Gardens," Geoffrey threw in, recovering from the shock of Audacia's altered looks, "so a picnic was called for."

Leave-taking began, and it so chanced that Lord Greydon fell in step beside Audacia as they walked from the salon. "I daresay you consider Kensington a large enough area to assure the safety of your feet," Audacia quipped. "I wonder at your daring in consenting to my company."

"For a friend such as Geoffrey I have braved many lesser dangers," Greydon replied, the hint of a humorous twinkle in his eye, "and could not in honor shrink from this greater one."

"Then perhaps you should consider tempering your friendship, for can one be called friend who foists such an onerous task upon you?" Audacia returned coldly, her color rising at his lordship's implication.

"Even onerous tasks may have hidden . . . rewards," the earl noted gravely, bringing Audacia to silence as she pondered his meaning.

"I congratulate you, Squire Webster . . . Geoffrey."

Lady Lucille smiled shyly as she handed him the apple she had just halved. "It was an excellent repast."

"If it pleased you, then I am well rewarded for my small efforts," he answered and paused to look closely at her before taking the apple.

Having grown steadily more aware of the interest the two had been exhibiting in each other as the day progressed, Audacia decided the supreme sacrifice was called for and spoke. "Lord Greydon, since it was you who chose the site of our luncheon, would you consent to show me more of the gardens?"

"After a feast such as we have enjoyed, ambling about could prove most beneficial," Greydon agreed with surprising speed, springing to his feet and holding out his hand to assist her rise.

A look of regret flickered across Lady Lucille's face as she made to rise also.

"No, sister," Lord Roland bantered. "With your birdish appetite you can have no need of exercise. Those among us who . . . enjoy food feel the need. Remain with Geoffrey, I am quite able to escort Miss Aderly." He ignored Audacia's answering frown and proffered his arm.

"Please do remain," Audacia added, "we shall manage." A warning smile was sent to Greydon. "I doubt that we shall have need of chaperonage with so many others present. The pace shall be slow . . . so as not to tire his lordship unduly," she ended archly, placing her hand on Greydon's arm.

"Will they ever have a friendly exchange?" Lady Lucille asked as the two walked away. "I know not if their bantering is genuine or feigned."

"I see it as a certain sign that they are interested in one another," the squire returned casually.

"Roland has shown an unusual tolerance for Audacia. Not outwardly, or even consciously, but . . . I fear I speak of matters you would rather let lie."

"What nonsense is that. I have noticed his interest," Geoffrey said and laughed.

"Are you distressed because of it?" she asked, lowering her eyes and plucking nervously at the grass upon which they sat.

"Distressed? No, I see no reason to be distressed. Audacia is levelheaded, despite the new coiffure," he said with a laugh, "and I'll trust she knows where her best interests lie. But let us speak of you. Did I not overhear Roland tell Audacia you spend some hours each week at the Chelsea Hospital?" he asked leaning forward. Tell me of your work," he said eagerly.

Lady Lucille's heart leapt. For the first time she dared to hope he might return her love once again.

Noticing that the neatly trimmed parallel hedges they were walking between concealed them from everyone in the gardens, Audacia removed her hand from Greydon's arm and halted.

The earl took a few more steps, then turned and gave her a questioning look as she squared her shoulders.

"My lord, I have endured your wit only for the sake of my friend and your sister. But we are now somewhat alone and as this shall, I trust, be a rare circumstance, I feel compelled to take exception to your quips given at my expense." Raising her skirts slightly, and gathering courage as he cocked an eyebrow at her, Audacia stalked forward and placed a well-aimed booted foot against his shins.

Shock, pain, then indignation played across his face. "I know you are far from ordinary, but I had not guessed you to be daft. Would you explain your action," Greydon demanded, taking a limping step toward her retreating figure.

"It is little enough for the—the enjoyment you had at my expense last winter," she retorted.

"Enjoyment? Our concepts of the pleasurable are vastly different, Miss Aderly," Greydon bit out, reaching down to rub his shin. "Taking a devil of a chill is no profitable reward for rescuing a very cold, wet 'lad.'"

A fierce blush came to Audacia's cheeks. "Am I to be forever taunted? Why do you not shout out to the world what you have done?" She waved her hand agitatedly, her voice rising. "Tell how you took advantage of . . ."

"I have never taken advantage of anyone." Greydon stalked forward prodded by a sudden surge of temper.

Courage fled as quickly as it had surged, and Audacia turned and ran. The earl followed, his long-legged lope much faster than her ragged, skirt-hampered run. Reaching her just as she came abreast a huge aged oak, he caught her shoulder with his large hand and spun her to face him. Both hands fastened her against the tree.

Trapped, Audacia's spirit rallied as she met his eyes. "Does a woman have to be unconscious for you to have your way with her?" she taunted.

He took in the swelling mounds of soft pink flesh revealed by the decolleté gown as Audacia stood gasping for breath. His eyes moved to her face. Raven wisps of curls formed a soft frame for flushed cheeks and gray, flashing eyes. Her look of defiance drew him. He bent his head to hers, and a long-contained, powerful emotion soared within him as his lips captured hers and his arms crushed her to him in an ardent embrace.

Without conscious thought, Audacia responded to his passion, her intensity matching his. But sudden awareness of her reaction to him shocked her and killed her response. She struggled to be free of his hold, confusion swelling within her.

Greydon drew back slowly but did not release her. His features contorted when he saw the anger and puzzled hurt upon her face, the tears welling in her eyes. His hands dropped as if scorched, and he fumbled at his pocket, drew a kerchief free, and handed it to her. "Audacia." His voice faltered. "I did—did not mean to . . ."

Turning her face from him, she bit her lip to stay the tears.

"I apologize," came stiffly.

The words strangely held no solace but caused a deeper pang, and she dared to look at him.

His grim face was proof of a new fear. "This shall not occur again," he told her coldly. "I ask that you forget it ever happened."

The coldness and the demeanor of his stance cut through her. A tightness gripped her throat. Dabbing her eyes dry, she gulped down a large lump. "We had best walk about for a time before we return," she managed through a dry throat. Easing past him, she continued walking.

The earl's visage was impassive but his every muscle was taut, and one fist clenched and unclenched as he followed.

170

* * *

"It is so good to be able to visit with you like this, Lucille," Geoffrey said as he gazed tenderly at her. "To be done with . . . with the awkwardness."

"It almost seems no time has passed . . . no," Lady Lucille amended, suddenly serious, "that is regrettably not true. Some lessons require time."

"There are moments when I wonder if I was not too . . . hasty seven years past," Geoffrey dared, watching her closely. "You are e'en more beautiful today than you were then." The idea suddenly came to him that she would not object to being kissed and he leaned forward, only to halt as he spied Audacia and Greydon coming near.

Wondering what had caused the squire to halt, Lady Lucille turned her head and breathed, "Drat," at the sight of the other two but hugged her new-found hope to her heart.

"What did you say?" Geoffrey asked, swinging his attention back to her.

"Nothing," she laughed lightly. "It does look as if they have had another disagreement," she added as she saw the set of her brother's face.

"Ending your stroll so soon?" Geoffrey called out, hopeful they would prolong it.

"Miss Aderly finds herself fatigued. Lucille, pack the hamper. We must return. You should also rest this afternoon," Greydon ordered.

"What is wrong?" Geoffrey rose and walked to Audacia. "You're as pale as a new moon. Why your hands are shaking," he said, taking hold of one. "What happened?" he demanded.

171

"Nothing, Geoffrey—truly. It is all the dancing and late evenings. Can we just go now?"

The squire looked distrustfully from Audacia to Greydon and disliked what he saw. "Of course," he told her. "Let me walk you to the landau." He put his arm about her protectively.

Lady Lucille watched the scene and felt her newly gladdened heart shake with fear. Her happiness seemed slowly to disappear at the sight of the squire's solicitous concern for Audacia and Roland's wincing spirit.

CHAPTER XVII

"Sir Maurice, how very good to see you," twittered Lady Darby. "You did receive my message?"

"Of course, and took it in good grace. Opera is not my passion as you well know," he answered accusingly.

"It was quite fortunate that Lady Mandel's box was not filled. We shall be sitting with them," she announced proudly. "The Mandel's daughter, Lady Lucille, and Audacia are becoming fast friends. Of course that opens so many doors," the viscountess ended smugly.

"Yes, yes. But how has Audacia taken to society? There was some concern on my part that . . ." Sir Maurice began.

"She has done marvelously," Lady Darby gushed, "and is so wise for her age. Why even Lord Greydon has paid her court, but she has eyes only for our Patrick. And he seems similarly inclined. Your dear Ann would have been so pleased I know, to see how matters are progressing between the two."

173

"Can't say the thought didn't rattle across my mind that the two might suit. I seem to recall them playing well together as children." Sir Maurice beamed happily at the prospect of his daughter being happily settled.

"Father!" Audacia called out as she entered the salon and flew to his arms.

"Why, my dear girl. You quite take my breath away. It has not been that long since we last saw each other," he blustered to hide his own emotions.

"A world away in time, Father," she replied, drawing back.

"You sound at odds, look a bit peaked. Is everything all right?" Sir Maurice asked, studying her carefully.

"Of course everything is well," Lady Darby said stepping between the two. "Merely the rigors of all the dancing and excitement, is it not, Audacia?"

"Yes, my lady," she answered softly.

"She is only excited because Patrick is coming with us to the opera. Ah, I believe I hear his voice now."

"Mother," young Darby said as he bowed, "and Sir Aderly. We rejoice that circumstances have brought you to London." He swaggered forward and offered his hand.

Sir Maurice's huge, work-stained hand covered the limp white fingers. He eyed the plump figure and mentally snorted. Lord Darby's seed had not bred true.

"Patrick has been showing your son about London," the viscountess continued to prattle.

"Daniel? Have you seen him this day? He was not at Lord Hillern's quarters and I've had no reply from the message I had Ballin take there this afternoon." His large shoulders shrugged. "Not that I'm concerned. Daniel did not know I was to be in London."

174

"Oh, you are not to worry, Sir Maurice. I am certain Patrick has taken excellent care of Daniel. One never knows what exploits a young lad will fall into, but Patrick"—she took his arm and gazed at him proudly—"will have seen that no harm has befallen him."

Smiling despite his displeasure at his mother's heavily sweetened manner, Darby waved a hand languidly. "Daniel was at Tattersall's with Hillern this morn. I believe they meant to drive to Dartford to test a new pair the viscount purchased. They will likely return in the morn. Hillern always travels pleasurably." He raised a brow to show his approval of this.

"Had hoped to see him this eve," the baronet said unhappily, "but you and I shall have a good visit." He patted Audacia's arm. "What has happened to your hair?" he blurted as he realized why she appeared so different to him. "And that gown?" Sir Maurice's eyes swept to Lady Darby. "Is it not rather too . . . ?"

"Fathers," twittered Lady Darby. "You are all alike. I imagine Lord Darby will take on such airs when our Helene is of an age," she dismissed his objections.

"Patrick, order the coach. It will be good to arrive at the opera before the crush."

"I see Sir Aderly has come to town. Now I wonder what prompted that?" Geoffrey spoke aloud as he gazed from Lord Greydon's box across to Lord and Lady Mandel's. "At least he seems to be making Lady Lucille smile. Why has she turned so glum?" he turned to Greydon. "Did she say anything that indicated I had displeased her?"

"You forget, I did not speak with my sister apart from you," the earl noted with a dry smile. The squire had mentioned Lucille or asked about her more oft since they had left her at his mother's than any time prior, even seven years past. Greydon took this for a good sign but could not rid himself of the feeling that his friend's heart was pledged elsewhere. As he glanced to his mother's box his eyes chanced to meet Audacia's. Their gaze held until her father spoke to her.

"Why don't we walk about after the next act. I think you would enjoy a chat with Sir Aderly, forthright fellow. Hope he's sense enough to put some distance between Audacia and that Darby fellow. See how that fop is dressed this eve? Did you ever see such a color, puce, perhaps? Uncomely as foul weather. Even your black is less offensive," Geoffrey noted taking in the earl's overly sombre black evening dress.

"You object to Darby?" Greydon questioned casually.

"Would you not object if that jackanapes was lollygagging near your sister?" the squire shot back. "Gad, man, think of what he is."

"I think I should like to meet the baronet. It would give you an opportunity to speak with . . . Audacia," Greydon offered.

A smile lit Geoffrey's features as his eyes went back to the Mandel box. "Yes, I have not had as much time with . . . her as I would like since I arrived. Let us go now; there is ample time, and if not, there will be seats enough when the other visitors leave the box. Come."

"Those two young men are a good study for what is best in England," Sir Aderly noted firmly after Lord Greydon and Squire Webster had left the box following the end of the act. "Your brother has a firm hand, Lady Lucille, and his looks are as pleasing as Squire Webster's, wouldn't you agree?"

A tinge of red came to her cheeks. "Both are considered handsome by the eligibles, I believe," she answered softly.

"The 'eligibles.'" The baronet gave a hearty chuckle. "But come, my lady, are you not one?" he teased. "I do believe the squire is partial to you."

Lady Lucille's face flamed red and she fanned herself agitatedly. "That is an unkind jest, sir," she said, rising. "Mr. Darby, would you be so kind as to escort me to the refreshments?"

Sir Aderly looked on in confusion as Patrick leaped to his feet, and in seconds the two were gone.

"I shall go with them." Lady Darby rose also. Sir Aderly's failure to include her son in his praise had not suited her, and she deemed it fitting punishment to deprive them of her company for a time.

"I apologize, Lady Mandel," he began after the viscountess's departure. "I had no intention . . ."

"No offense given or taken," the marchioness assured him. "My daughter is unusually sensitive about Geoffrey still."

He nodded with shared understanding. "An old man tends to be clumsy," he sighed. "I had hoped a better ending for the pair."

"As I also did." She smiled sadly. "But tell me more of your work. Will it truly be a boon for owners as well as tenants? Lord Mandel will wish to know all."

The conversation flowed unheard past Audacia. She had been withdrawn since Greydon's entrance into the box. How can he act so coldly? she asked herself repeatedly. I should tell father. Tell him what? her mind teased.

Seeking safer, less turmoil-ridden ground, she turned her attention to her plans for Geoffrey. Something was clearly amiss there, for Lady Lucille's eager interest of the morn, which had shown such promise, was but apathetic indifference now. Audacia felt like shaking the older girl, for it was clear to her that Geoffrey loved Lord Greydon's sister and the match was suitable on all grounds.

The exchange between the marchioness and her father puzzled her. Apparently there was more between the squire and Lucille than she knew of. But when? Geoffrey had not been to London for almost eight years except for occasional business dealings. Was Lady Lucille the reason for his absence?

"My dear, are you quite all right?" Lady Mandel asked her. "You have the strangest look. Do you feel faint?"

"No. No, my lady." She jerked her attention from the thought that had just burst through her mental haze. "I feel fine."

Sir Maurice rubbed his chin thoughtfully. He had seen such looks before, and never had they presaged an uneventful time for him.

"Yes." Lady Darby's voice preceded her into the box. "Isn't Patrick thoughtful, insisting upon bringing Audacia an ice. Of course, you know he thinks the world of her." Her confidential tone was belied by its volume. "But then, I shan't want to spoil their surprise." She tripped lightly into their midst, a beaming smile announcing that she had forgiven all. After all, she reasoned, everything is going so well.

"Are you warm enough? The night air is damp," Lord

178

Greydon said as he handed his sister into his high-perch phaeton.

"Believe me, Roland, I shall enjoy the air. Mr. Darby is almost more than one can bear. I pleaded the headache and fatigue only to escape."

"It was a sham?"

"It was the only way I could see to manage it so that we could have some time alone. You do not mind?"

With a shake of his head, he flicked the reins and said, "What is in that devious head of yours that requires such privacy?" His teasing smile faded as he glanced to her and saw that tears were slowly rolling down her cheeks. "Speak of what troubles you," he urged gently.

Lady Lucille angrily dabbed the tears away. "I do not mean to make a scene," she promised and blew her nose. "It is all rather simple. I wish your aid in helping Geoffrey achieve a match with Audacia." She hurried her words before courage should fail.

"A match between them? Surely you cannot mean that? Why, you are in . . ." He stole another look at his sister and ended, "Why?"

"You have seen the care, the concern he shows for her. They both brighten when they see each other. You cannot deny it," Lady Lucille rushed on. "My chance was lost long ago when I proved unworthy. No, do not interrupt me," she silenced his objection. "I have never spoken of what occurred between Geoffrey and myself then and I will not do so now. Only believe what I say."

Slowly Greydon nodded.

"You cannot disclaim he cares for her, can you?" she asked, her heart breaking that she had to force this.

Numbly, he nodded again.

"I am so sorry, Roland, but we owe him this. With Audacia at his side he would be happy. You have seen how she was able to bring life back to him after we failed. Won't you help?"

The conflict between guilt and personal desires, his uncertainty and what he perceived as fact, bruised Greydon's heart and mind, but in the end he nodded once again.

Audacia was almost thankful to Lady Darby for having maneuvered her into this walk with Patrick on the lantern-lit paths at Covent Garden, where their party had gone to sup after the opera. He had proven pleasingly silent, thus freeing her to dwell on Lord Greydon. She had felt the earl's haunted, brooding eyes had been upon her oft this eve. Her heart longed for a way to free him from a torment no one else seemed to sense.

"What are your thoughts, Miss Aderly?" Darby asked, watching Audacia, trying to gauge if the time was opportune for him to bring matters between them to agreement.

"I was thinking of Lady Lucille and Squire Webster," she answered, bringing the pair who were not far from her thoughts to the fore. "Do you think they suit?"

"Each other?" Patrick asked in surprise.

"Who else?" Audacia laughed.

"They are of a like age, now that you speak of it I think it a capital idea," he answered, beaming, a question that had troubled him amply answered by her suggestion.

"Good, then you will be willing to help?"

"Anything to please you, but how, Audacia?"

The possessive tone he used sent a warning through her. "I think we should return now."

. "Let us walk on for a short space. There is so much I would speak of," Patrick urged smoothly.

"We can have little to say to one another that cannot be said in the presence of all, Mr. Darby." Her tone sharpened as his hand continued to press her forward.

"You wish my aid in the squire's cause. I can do much for him. You saw how Lady Lucille listened, hung upon my every word. Why, I have her in my pocket," he preened and moved his hand to capture hers.

"Please release me," she said softly, anger winning over fear as she realized they were alone on the dimly lit walk.

"My dear," he protested, grabbing her other hand, "you must realize how I feel about you. It has been no secret. Even your father agrees a match between us is ideal," he said, drawing her closer.

"You have no reason to speak thus to me," she said loudly. "I have offered you no encouragement. Release me or I shall scream."

"As you wish. Scream all you like. Here it shall not be heeded. Do you think me a fool? Come, my sweet, relax and you shall enjoy this as much as I." The strength of the pompous dandy surprised and alarmed Audacia.

"No," she screamed. "No!" And she began kicking and struggling with all her might.

" 'Tis unwise for you to anger me," Darby spat, "for it puts me of a mind not to be gentle. You shall learn your lesson." Twisting her arm, he tightened his hold.

The pain cleared Audacia's mind of any objections to any action on her part. She stopped struggling in hopes he would grant her an opening. The sound of running steps stiffened both.

In a second Darby's hands were wrenched from her by

a dark, tall, looming figure of a man. Flesh and bone met in a dull muffled thud as a fist relieved Patrick of consciousness.

The dim light half concealed her rescuer's features, but Audacia recognized Lord Greydon's stance. Her heart leapt. She trembled, realizing he had but to open his arms for her to surrender to their embrace.

"Are you witless to go walking about alone with every man you know?" he asked, anger masking his concern.

"I could have managed by myself," she half cried; fear, anger, and disappointment took her remaining equilibrium. "I hardly needed *you.*"

Greydon started as if slapped. "I see," he breathed slowly. "Are you unhurt?" came after a pause.

"Only my arm is bruised, just a bruise. What of him?" she asked, the near hysteria in her voice beginning to fade.

"More unharmed than I would have him," Greydon said contemptuously. "If you feel you can, we should return to your party," he suggested tonelessly.

With a nod, she began to walk slowly forward. Greydon's silent company as he followed close behind was a strange comfort to her, but the words Audacia overheard him speak a short time later in an aside to Geoffrey took away the little warmth she had found. "You had best hurry your 'lad' to the safety of Warwickshire. You are for each other and the country."

CHAPTER XVIII

Rain drizzled down the windows of the morning room at No. 31 Mount Street. Clouds had darkened the sky from early morn, reflecting the mood within.

"Why don't we dress as boys and go about in the rain?" Helene suggested, bouncing into the room.

"I should never have told you of my wicked ways." Audacia smiled vaguely and laid aside the unread magazine she held. "The weather is so dismal," she sighed, rose and walked to the windows.

"Everyone has been so downcast of late," Helene bemoaned, plopping into a chair. "Hardly any of you are even civil anymore."

"Your mother has been critical again?" Audacia asked vacantly, still staring at the rain-soaked street.

"She has not been. That is what worries me," the young girl returned. "When Mother forgets to find fault with me

183

she is truly worried. Do you know what could occupy her so, Audee?"

"Why, no. I haven't noticed anything unusual. Look, a hansom is halting at our door." She pressed her nose to the glass. "It's Geoffrey. Excellent," Audacia brightened. "Now, please, Helene, I must speak to Squire Webster alone."

"Will you let us dress as boys and go about the park?" Helene demanded irritably, thinking no one was the least interested in her. I hope I never grow up, she thought as she awaited the reply. Even Audacia is no longer any fun.

"All right, anything," Audacia whispered as she heard the butler's steps. "Go as soon as Trotter is out of sight and warn me if your mother returns."

Geoffrey's posture was as limp as the dampened cloak he handed the butler before glumly following him to the morning room. For him the presence of the youngest Darby was a relief, for Audacia was certain to object when she learned his reason for coming.

But the squire's respite was brief, for true to her bargain, Helene slipped from the morning room as the sound of Trotter's footsteps faded.

"You have been neglecting me shamefully," Audacia challenged. "I know you were invited to Salver's ball this Thursday past and you let me be prey of all the fops and dandies. There has been no opportunity to speak with you since I saw you last at Covent Garden with Lady Mandel's party," she complained.

"Speaking of that, what was it that happened to young Darby? There is a rumor about that a very blackened eye is keeping him close to his rooms this past week. You wouldn't be responsible for that?"

"Why would I have reason to do such a thing?" Audacia asked irritably. "It is you I wish to speak of."

"First let me tell you I have decided to return to Web Hall."

"But you can't," she protested in dismay.

"There is no reason for me to remain here," he returned with finality.

Concern wrinkled Audacia's brow as she slowly sank into a chair.

"I shall look forward to your return to Bedworth," Geoffrey added as he sat across from her, visibly relieved that she had not flown into high whoops.

"Before your arm was lost," Audacia said as she watched him closely, "did you mean to wed Lady Lucille?"

A long stare preceded the squire's answer. "There is little you did not know of me. I suppose you have guessed that?" A dry, chilling chuckle followed her answering nod. "It is true." A look of the old bitterness washed over him. "When I came back from Portugal I was no longer a 'whole' man. Neither she nor I could adjust to it."

"So you fled to your country home, prepared to spend the rest of your life wallowing in self-pity."

"But a certain young miss wouldn't have it that way." A smile came despite the dour emotions that filled him. "It is you I should have wed," he said half seriously.

Audacia straightened stiffly in the chair. "I have never heard such nonsense. Why wed someone who does not love you when you can have another who does?"

Rising, Geoffrey bowed, preparing to take leave.

"Lady Lucille loves you very much," Audacia told him calmly.

"That has been very well hidden from me," burst from the squire. "One moment she is smiling at me and the next I could be in Warwick for all the attention I get. And Warwickshire is exactly where I intend to be."

"But Geoffrey." Audacia laid a hand on his arm to stay him. "Have you not thought that she may be in as much doubt regarding the direction of your affections. What is she to think when you suddenly return after years of absence? Have you spoken to her of your attachment?"

"How can I when she pales at the very mention of the arm? I . . . you have accepted it, but she still regards me as only part a man. No, Audacia . . ."

"Then you must make her accept it. Show her what little effect it has had."

"If she would consent to wed me, it would be from pity." Geoffrey voiced the true hindering fear at last. "I could not abide knowing she forced herself to look upon me, to touch me and not . . ." He turned from her.

Tears came to Audacia's eyes at the pain she saw upon her friend. Her resolve tightened. "I know she loves you, Geoffrey. You should not toss aside happiness so foolishly. Give her a chance. Give yourself a chance. Remain a few weeks more, please?"

"There will only be more hurt."

"That is what you said when first we met and I told you that you could do most things that men do. I was not willing to pity you then, nor now." She toughened her tone. "Perhaps your love is not strong enough for the test?"

A wry smile came to the squire's lips. "I have never understood how you manage to make things look proba-ble."

186

"*Obstinacy* was a word you used in the past," she said and smiled in return.

"Three weeks more, that is all," he conceded.

"But you must act the suitor," Audacia prompted. "Remove any doubt from Lady Lucille's mind as to your intentions—if they be honorable." She winked.

"Questions do begin to enter my mind," said the squire and tilted his head at the eager figure before him. "With all this talk of what I must do what is it you shall do?"

A nervous laugh answered him. "I shall extol your virtues to the lady."

"About Roland," Geoffrey persisted, beginning to enjoy himself.

"Other than wondering at Lady Lucille's charming ways after being afflicted with Lord Greydon's willful, pigheaded, pretentious behavior, I think not of the gentleman," Audacia said, folding her arms, a stubborn glint entering her eyes.

"How unfortunate," the squire noted innocently. "I had thought you charmed him mightily."

"Are you certain you would rather come with us?" Sir Aderly asked Audacia after Lady Darby's startled look at the suggestion that she ride in his hired coach to the Saltouns' ball.

"With my father and brother to escort me, I lack nothing," she replied. "We have had so little time together," she added, turning to the viscountess, "and surely you welcome a few moments alone with Mr. Darby since Lord Darby is unable to attend?"

"Patrick will be so disappointed," Lady Darby said

pointedly, "but he will understand your wish to attend with your father.

"Daniel, do you know what could be delaying his arrival?" she asked the younger Aderly.

"No. No," Audacia's brother answered nervously. "Could we not depart now, Father?" he asked.

A frown at his son's rudeness was tempered as Sir Aderly bowed to Lady Darby. "You will forgive Daniel's impatience, my lady," he apologized. "The young," Sir Maurice said with an explanatory lift of his brow.

"Oh, yes," Lady Darby sighed. "I am so fortunate in my Patrick. Do not hesitate on my part. We shall follow directly," she added lightly. "Fill Patrick's name in on your dance card, Audacia," the viscountess admonished. "He would be crushed if you do not."

Curtsying lightly, Audacia murmured noncommittally as she walked past her; the viscountess's words reminded her to make certain her card was entirely filled before Mr. Darby could arrive.

Once in the coach, Sir Aderly began a rapid questioning of Daniel's opinion of London, since this was his first opportunity to visit with his son. When Daniel displayed little enthusiasm and more lack of knowledge, he paused.

Sensing trouble brewing, Audacia began a stream of lively chatter, imparting the more humorous incidents Helene had involved her in or had subjected the family to during her visit.

Her father continued to study Daniel, who sat staring at his hands, which clenched and unclenched. Receiving no reaction from either, Audacia's stories trailed off unfinished.

Only street noises were sounding about them when

Daniel blurted angrily, "There is no reason I should not enjoy my stay here. Why should I be required to visit those stuffy acquaintences of yours and speak of laws and machinery and . . ." His voice faded into silence.

"What has young Darby been filling you with?" Sir Maurice asked sharply. "It was understood your studies were not to be laid aside entirely while here, but broadened by men of experience. You are not yourself, my son. What has altered you so?"

"How would you know if I have changed?" the young man flung back. "With your head forever with your machines."

"Daniel!" Audacia exclaimed.

"And who are you to speak?" he threw heatedly at her, "treating Mr. Darby so callously. Why you are little better than a teasing—"

"I'll not have you speak to your sister thus," Sir Aderly cut him off. "Tomorrow you are to come to my rooms and we shall discuss what has wrought such ill change in your mien."

Daniel stared belligerently for a moment, then dropped his head. When the coach slowed because of the crush of vehicles approaching to attend the ball, he jumped from it and ran into the crowd of beggars, vendors, and sight-seeking commoners.

"Father, should you not go after him?" Audacia asked concernedly. "This is so unlike him. He must be ill."

"The night air will cool his temper." Worry lines eased on the baronet's face as he chuckled.

"Father?" Audacia asked at this strange reaction.

"I should have guessed what is upsetting your brother. Daniel probably fears that I shall learn that he spent an evening imbibing too freely, and enjoying other libertine pleasures. I will assure him my youth is not entirely forgotten. But we have arrived. Do not concern yourself overly much about him—pangs of manhood," Sir Maurice sought to assure his daughter.

Audacia nodded, but doubt lingered. What had Darby told him that he accused her of untoward actions? The matter would have to be discussed later; this eve she hoped to advance the squire's cause.

Audacia glanced about the ballroom and spied Lady Lucille's royal green gown. Having just directed Geoffrey to the gardens, she was eager to complete her strategy. "Lady Greydon," she began, joining her.

"Lucille, as we agreed," her ladyship corrected, smiling. "And thank you for sending me these hair ribbons. I forgot to mention how delighted I was with them when we arrived. It is the perfect shade for my gown. So kind of you."

"I knew they would match the moment I saw them at the Emporium."

"I am thankful I showed you this gown when you called with the viscountess." She laid her gloved hand on Audacia's arm. "It has been a long time since I have had the pleasure of a coz such as we had that morn."

"I am hopeful we shall prove good friends," Audacia said, thinking of how much she would enjoy Lucille's company if she and the squire wed.

"Then we must, for I feel the same," her ladyship squeezed her hand. "But I interrupted you. What was it you wished?"

"Oh, yes. I discovered the most unusual statue at the far

end of the gardens. Won't you come and look at it? I am certain you shall be able to tell me what it is."

"Of course. It will be a pleasure to escape the heat of this crush."

"I must speak with my father for just a moment. Do go ahead. I shall join you."

"Was that my sister who just went outdoors?" Lord Greydon asked Audacia, pausing at her side.

"Why, no," she lied. "Lady Lucille has retired to the upper floor to refresh herself."

"Have you seen Geoff?"

"In the card rooms, I believe. He was being plagued by matrons wishing to dance with him."

"Geoff would never go to the card rooms to avoid them. I think I shall check the gardens," Greydon told her doubtfully.

"I assure you neither one is there," she repeated, biting her tongue to keep from speaking her true thoughts about his interference.

A suspicious glint came to the earl's eyes as he studied her. "We are being unusually pleasant this eve," he noted warily.

"And 'we' are being unusually meddlesome."

"I was incorrect, excuse me," Greydon inclined his head. "You are your usual disagreeable self."

"Which says little for your priggish charm," Audacia tossed back with a smile.

"But a dissembler I am not."

"You accuse me, my lord?"

"Let us walk. We attract more attention than is to my liking." He noted those about beginning to glance at them frequently.

"In the gardens, my lord? I was cautioned against venturing forth unchaperoned. But he who warned me knows I take little heed of his words," she added, seeing he was determined to enter the gardens either with her or alone. "I am told there is a fountain in the center," she said. "Could you lead me there," Audacia stalled for time thinking how fortunate she had been in directing Geoffrey and Lady Lucille to a different area.

Greydon proffered his arm. "I wonder that you dare," he quoted her words archly.

Meeting his eyes as she laid a hand upon his arm, Audacia's heart skipped a beat. "If only" echoed through her mind. Silence escorted them till they halted before the softly spraying fountain. A golden half-moon hung in the sky overhead and soft strains of a waltz drifted through the neatly trimmed shrubs. A profusion of spring flowers scented the air.

The spell of enchantment that hung over them as they walked slowly forward was broken by Greydon's words. "What have you been about this eve?" he asked softly, gazing down at her profile and finding he was barely able to restrain himself from reaching out to brush back a black wisp that had gone astray and curled softly against her cheek.

"About?" Her gentle tone matched his, then a warning pushed its way into her thoughts. "What do you mean, my lord?" she asked guilelessly, halting.

"My sister has done you no harm. Why do you wish to cause her pain?"

Shock washed the affection from Audacia's features. "I would do nothing to harm Lady Lucille," she protested.

192

"Then it is Geoffrey you wish to punish?" Greydon asked, even more condemningly.

"Speak plainly, my lord," she demanded.

"It has been clear all evening that you were doing your utmost to throw Lucille and Geoffrey together."

"And achieving it seldom because of your interference," Audacia returned sharply. "I can add *dolt* to the list of your qualities, my lord." She stepped closer to him in her anger.

Greydon moved back, halting just in front of the prickly hedge marking the path. "And I *malicious* to yours. Lucille has suffered enough because of her feelings for Geoff. But then you know that."

"She does love him!" Audacia clapped her hands in delight at the new information.

"And it speaks little but ill of you that you should toss him in her path at every step. And all when you shall wed him," Greydon bit out.

Her joyous expression became frozen. Slowly her hands settled to her side. "You believe me to be toying with Geoffrey's affections?"

"Never more heartless a wench have I seen."

"Words fail me, my lord," Audacia answered slowly. "You truly believe this of me?"

His damning look answered her.

Anger and pain flared. "You—you contemptible fool!" she cried out and gave him a mighty push.

Totally off guard, Greydon found himself falling backward into the spiny hedge. A sound strangely like a sob came to his ears as the bush's thorns added to his anguish.

CHAPTER XIX

The hansom halted before Lord Mandel's residence, and the driver waited patiently for the disagreement within the vehicle to end.

"We should wait for you," Miss Bea was objecting.

"I should like to come in," Helene put in.

"Both of you are to go on to the park. Here is the money for the driver. I will join you as soon as I can," Audacia told them firmly.

"Her ladyship will be most displeased," the abigail warned.

"That I make a morning call on Lady Greydon? Nonsense, Miss Bea. Helene, stop your pouting and enjoy a good romp."

"But you promised we would . . ."

"And we shall," the other cut her off quickly lest Miss Bea discover what she had promised. Giving the young girl's hand a squeeze, she pledged, "Plans must be made first."

"Plans for what?" Miss Strowne asked suspiciously.

"For a picnic," her charge returned lightly and stepped from the coach before further could be asked.

"We shall wait to see if you are admitted," the abigail called from the cab.

A stern-faced butler opened the Mandels' door at Audacia's knock.

"Miss Aderly to see Lady Greydon," she told him crisply.

"One moment, miss." The butler motioned a footman to stand watch over the open door and disappeared. He returned a short time later and bowed. "Roberts shall show you to the Blue Salon, miss."

The footman led the way through the ornately decorated corridor, up the delicately carved stairs, to a room located midway on the second floor. Done in shades of blue, the salon had a cool, relaxed air. Audacia was relieved to see that Lady Lucille was alone.

"Good morn." Lady Lucille greeted her caller more coolly than usual.

"I come to speak with you because . . . because I fear you may be under a false impression regarding me," Audacia said hesitantly.

"That was corrected last eve, was it not?"

After puzzling the words briefly, Audacia asked, "Geoffrey spoke with you of me?"

Lady Lucille blanched. "I was speaking of your impertinent treatment of my brother."

A blush brushed tinges of red across Audacia's face. "That was a thoughtless action on my part," she stated slowly. "But the words that prompted it are the reason for my coming today. I fear you may think as Lord Greydon does. Please listen to what I have to say," she entreated. "Your happiness depends upon it."

"I think that highly unlikely."

"Geoffrey Webster loves you, my lady," Audacia said, ignoring the other's assumed hauteur. "He has a right to . . ."

"You have no *right* to speak to me of this," Lady Lucille rose agitatedly.

"Have you no love for him? Have his thoughts that you feel only pity for him been true?" Audacia challenged.

"I shall not discuss this matter. Please go."

"Lady Lucille, I come as a friend. I desire nothing more than Geoffrey's happiness and yours," she continued to plead. "He believes you cannot love him because he is no longer a whole man. I cannot think so little of you to credit the thought that the loss of his arm made him less a man to you. Surely you see that he is whole in his being. He is a loving, feeling man and he needs your love."

Tears coursed down the other's face. "I have . . . seen him . . . with you. It is you . . . who . . . brings a smile to his face. I am no longer held highly in his affections."

"Geoffrey does not love me. If he does it is only as a—a sister . . . as a friend. He feels gratitude because I would not pity him."

"He loves you and you must wed him. He deserves that much from life," Lucille repeated stubbornly.

"I do not love him. What happiness would there be? It is *you* who holds his heart. Only open yours for him," she urged, laying a hand on the other's trembling shoulders.

Sensing the compassion and sincerity that prompted

Audacia's words, Lady Lucille accepted her shoulder and sobbed openly.

After the first burst of emotion had passed, Audacia led her to the sofa and they sat down.

"It is you he must wed," Lady Lucille insisted still. "I would bring him nothing but pain, and I do so wish to see him happy."

"Then do nothing. Be neither too cool nor too doting when Geoffrey is near. If you observe him closely you will soon see it is not I he cares for."

Lady Lucille gave a sad shake to her head and dabbed the last tears from her eyes. "Even if what you say is true, I could never convince him that his lost arm matters not to me."

"Can we be friends again?" Audacia asked, while absorbing her words. "Even though Lord Greydon despises me?"

A chuckle broke from Lady Lucille. "It was a set down he has deserved for years," she said laughing and crying together. "How did you dare do it?"

Ruefulness marked Audacia. "In truth, it was done without thought." She shrugged, a forlorn look coming to her features. "My temper has not oft been so liable to run me to ruin. Indeed, I have puzzled long over . . ."

"Puzzled over what?" Lucille prompted.

"Why Lord Greydon sets my ire aflame. It seems we must cross swords when we meet, even when I resolve not to."

Lady Lucille started. "Oh, dear. He is to call upon me shortly. You had best go, for I could not foreswear what his temper will show so soon after insult. Vastly out of spirits was he last eve, although few saw the incident."

"I care not to bring his retribution upon my head," Audacia agreed. "I will be off, but you will consider what I have spoken of?"

"Yes, and if I can calm Roland, mayhaps we can all go riding on the morrow?"

"But I have no mount."

"Never fear, Father has a stable full. I shall send word. Good day, dear friend. If only it could be as you say." Lady Lucille kissed Audacia lightly on the cheek and the two embraced. "I had better walk with you . . . in case Roland should appear."

They ambled slowly through the corridor and down the stairs. At the foot of the steps a deep voice reached them. Turning to each other in alarm, they broke into nervous giggles that nearly gave them away. "This way." Lady Lucille grabbed Audacia's hand and pulled her towards a door. "Inside." She pulled the door shut just as Greydon came around the corner.

"Good morn, brother."

"Blast the morn," he snapped irritably.

"You aren't still suffering from the thorns, are you?" she asked repressing a smile. "Mayhaps it is just an ill humor."

A withering look was cast her way. "My health is excellent. But Miss Aderly's shall not be if I chance to meet her. If she were a lad . . ."

"But alas, she is not," Lady Lucille interrupted. "Perhaps you should not think so harshly of her, Roland."

"Never was a woman more deserving of it."

"Let us not stand about chatting for all to hear. I will come to the Blue Salon in a few moments. There is a matter I must attend first."

With an answering nod he turned and stalked up the stairs.

"He is gone," Lady Lucille whispered. "Can you find the door? Good. I will send a note to you this afternoon."

With a wave of farewell, Audacia hastened to the doors. A sigh escaped her as she settled into the hansom, her fears of encountering Lord Greydon relieved.

"I thought I might find you here," Squire Webster greeted Audacia as she, Helene, and Miss Strowne strolled in St. James Park. "May I walk with you?"

"Of course, squire," Helene smiled. "Tell me, have you danced much of late?"

"Ah, more than I would have wished," he said and smiled in return. "My feet weary of the demands made upon them and they guide me to card rooms instead of assemblies. But then, a beauty such as yours has not been present."

Helene blushed, a beaming smile revealing her pleasure.

"And you, Miss Aderly. How do you fare this morn? I have heard a strange tale that a certain lord wishes his acquaintence with you did not involve quite as much . . . Well, let us say his spirit has been somewhat pricked."

"What an odd thing to say. Audee, what can it mean?" Helene asked.

"A gentleman's nonsense," Audacia said, a blush denying a total innocence of its meaning. "Geoffrey, there is something I would have you do," she gladly changed the conversation's trend.

"Only *one* something?" he parried.

A frown dismissed his tease. "Please speak with Daniel." She glanced from the squire to Miss Bea and Helene.

199

"Let us walk forward a pace." When the distance was sufficient, she continued. "I am very concerned about him. He has been so little near me and when he is, he is as nervous as a man about to be condemned. Father believes it has something to do with boyish pranks . . ."

"But you do not?"

"Daniel has always confided in me when troubled. I cannot but feel this is something very serious. He may be willing to speak more openly with—with you. Will you do this for me?"

"I'll stop by his quarters after I leave you, if you but give me their direction," he assured her. "Come now, smile. I may fail with the gentler sex but with Daniel I shall succeed."

"You have not failed," Audacia said pointedly, "with anyone just yet. Persistence shall bring success."

"In that case, mayhaps I would do well to warn that particular gentleman I mentioned. He would do well to leave London if he values the safety of his life, for I know no one more persistent than you," he teased.

"More nonsense," came the clipped reply. "We *shall* excuse you, Squire Webster." A weary smile forgave him. "Do see Daniel," Audacia urged even as she pondered what caused her concern for him to grow.

"I find you at last," young Darby greeted Daniel Aderly. "Has it been your intention to elude me? Only Hillern's chance guess brought me here."

"Why should I not wish to see you, Patrick?" Daniel asked nervously.

"Only you could answer that," the other returned flicking his gloves casually atop the table and sitting. "What a mundane establishment," he noted sarcastically. "I believed I had taught you better. Surely you do not mean to drink that swill?"

Daniel raised the mug and quaffed the remainder of the ale as if to dare him.

"Hillern and I are going to Waitier's this eve. Shall you accompany us?" Darby asked as his eyes took in the soot-stained timbers of the tavern and dismissed its inhabitants as vulgar. "Will you?" he repeated.

As Daniel surveyed the dregs of his mug, his nervousness turned to gloom. "You know I have no more funds. How am I to pay the notes you already hold?"

"Who would ask a 'brother' for payment?" Patrick leaned back and viewed the dismal lad smugly.

"Brother? But I am no kin of yours," Daniel leaned forward, seeing a glimmer of hope in Darby's attitude.

"In blood, no. But marriage could make us so. Speak with your sister. Tell her the advantages of making a match with me."

"If I did this you would not demand payment?" Daniel asked eagerly.

"There would be no reason to," the other smiled.

Relief flooded the young lad's features, then ebbed away. "But what if Audacia is unwilling? I mean, she may have a *tendre* for another."

"I am certain you shall find a way to convince her my suit is worthy," Darby said, the edge of his voice warningly clear. "But if you wish"—he shrugged insolently—"I would be willing to give you one last loan with which you may regain your fortunes. Luck cannot desert you forever."

"I may play where I wish and what I wish?" Daniel asked as he weighed the offer.

"If you wish, I shan't even attend you this eve," Patrick scoffed.

"No, I did not mean that." He adjusted his limp, crushed cravat nervously. "I shall do it," burst from him as he struggled with the decision. Gambling fever sprang to his eyes with the surrender of reason. All was forgotten as he greedily snatched the bills Darby had drawn from his pocket.

CHAPTER XX

Pleading a headache, Audacia was able to retire early in the eve. Once in her room, she began to pace about. After some time had passed she was forced to bemoan the lack of a worthy idea. There has to be some way, she thought, some way to assure both Geoffrey and Lucille of each other's affection.

"May I come in?" Helene whispered, peeking into the room. "I thought we might lay our plans."

"Plans? Oh, yes. But not this eve. I must find a solution for Squire Webster's problem first."

"What problem does he have? Are the matrons still treading on his toes?"

Audacia studied the young girl. "This is serious and must be a secret between you and me," she cautioned.

"A secret? I love secrets. Tell me all," Helene appealed, sitting upon the bed.

Joining her, Audacia hesitated to speak.

"I promise I shall not tell anyone," the other reassured her earnestly.

"All right. You see, Helene, Squire Webster is in love with Lady Lucille Greydon, and she also with him."

"Then there is no problem," the other stated brightly.

"But there is," Audacia returned, "and I cannot think of a way to resolve it. Geoffrey believes Lady Lucille merely pities him and Lady Lucille thinks he no longer cares for her."

"Why not simply tell them they are wrong?"

"I have attempted that. No, one must be more devious than to use the truth with these two." Audacia frowned. "If only Geoffrey could be assured . . ."

"Has all this been caused because he lost his arm?" Helene asked, the thought just now dawning.

"That is, sadly, the hub of the matter."

"Then the answer lies plainly before you."

"My mind is befuddled then, for I see no answer. Pray, tell me, what is it that you think would suit?"

"Squire Webster thinks Lady Lucille pities him, so the thing to do is to have him do something which would make him a hero in her eyes," Helene said matter-of-factly. "That would give him the confidence to press his suit."

"But what could we do to cause that?" Audacia dismissed the idea with a wave of her hand.

"I don't think it is a foolish idea," Helene protested. "Why couldn't we start a rumor that the squire rescued someone?"

"Rescued whom? How could he . . . ?" The thought began to whirl through Audacia's mind. "Rescue," she repeated thoughtfully, more positively.

"Yes, we must invent a rumor that will be quickly spread.

"No, not a rumor. Think of the effect if Lady Lucille saw Geoffrey pull someone from harm's grasp." Audacia rose, her eyes sparkling brightly.

"But who? How?" It was Helene's turn to be puzzled.

"I think I know both who and how." Audacia smiled. "And when."

"You do?"

"Tomorrow. Don't you recall the note Lady Lucille sent? I am to go riding with her, and she said Geoffrey is to join us."

"What will you do?" Helene asked eagerly.

"Well, Lady Lucille has never seen me ride so it should be easy to convince her I cannot hold my seat." The idea was honed and refined as Audacia put it into words. "I only wish it was Lady Lucille being saved," she ended. "But I dare not chance that."

"I think the idea is superb. If only I could be there to see you," Helene lamented.

"You would consider it dull. Especially if I am success-ful. Then the two of them shall be in each other's pockets and notice no one else."

Helene wrinkled her nose in disgust, causing Audacia to laugh. "One day it will be the same for you," she told her and mentally crossed her fingers that tomorrow would see a happy conclusion for Geoffrey.

"It is a beautiful morn," Audacia chattered happily as the threesome came from the Darby's residence.

"And I the most fortunate of men to be in the company

of two such lovely women," Geoffrey offered gallantly as the footmen assisted the women atop their sidesaddles.

"Squire Webster told me you have ridden with him, so I chose one of the more lively geldings from the stable," Lady Lucille explained. "My Daisy is a gentle plodder, but that suits me. You and Squire Webster can canter ahead if you wish to take the edge from your mounts."

Struggling with the unaccustomed sidesaddle and skirts, Audacia had all she could handle. Once settled in, she glanced at Geoffrey, who was observing her with a broad grin across his face.

"I neglected to inform Lady Lucille of your usual mode of riding." His tone teased. He became serious as Audacia's gelding snorted, tossing its head and prancing nervously as they entered the more heavily trafficked street. "Can you handle the brute?"

"Never fear," she retorted, concentrating on controlling her mount. If this continues she thought, I will have little need of my hatpin.

At first she developed doubts about the safety of her purposed venture, but as she gradually became accustomed to the saddle and gained control over the gelding her confidence increased. Assured that her plan was feasible, Audacia began to enjoy the conversation.

"It is regrettable that Roland would not come," Lady Lucille noted, reveling in the early morning May sunshine.

"He may yet appear," Geoffrey told them.

"What!" exclaimed Audacia, worry creasing her face.

"Last eve he made mention of joining us. I believe he had an early morn appointment." The squire did not add that he and Greydon had spent the evening in search of young Daniel Aderly, nor that the earl meant to call at Hillern's address this morn.

"You have no reason to fear Roland, Audacia. He is a gentleman," Lady Lucille sought to reassure her, misreading her concern. "The incident with the hedge shall not be mentioned."

Nodding vaguely in response, Audacia surveyed the area before them. Few riders were in the park because of the early hour. A broad, open meadow lay before them.

Now is the time, she thought. With Pegasus beneath him, Geoffrey will have little trouble "saving" me from the disaster of a "bolting" mount. It could not be more perfect, she reasoned to herself. The gelding beneath her chose this moment to lurch forward and Audacia reined him in tightly, then fumbled with her bonnet as if to right it but secretly removed one of the pins holding it in place.

"With this clear avenue before us, mayhaps it would be wise to have a run. It would ease the handling of your steed to use some of his spirit," Geoffrey suggested.

"But Lady Lucille does not care to gallop," Audacia feigned protest, letting the gelding ease ahead so they would not see her prick him in order to affect the bolting. Getting a firm hold on the saddle, she plunged the hatpin home.

The gelding burst forward, nearly unseating Audacia. Dropping the pin, she clung to the saddle and mane, the necessity of deliverance no longer a pretense.

Daisy, Lady Lucille's gentle mare, had shied at the gelding's snorting; half-rearing it burst forward also. Geoffrey sought first to assure himself that she was under control.

"For Lord's sake, Geoffrey," Lady Lucille exclaimed, "Find someone to go after her. She'll be thrown."

Wheeling his mount to pursue the runaway, the squire dug his heels into Pegasus' flanks, his fear for Audacia overriding Lucille's words.

A huge black stallion reared to a halt before Lady Lucille as she watched the squire race away.

"What is about?" Greydon shouted, waving at the pair.

"The gelding I chose for Audacia has bolted. I told Geoffrey to find someone, but he has gone after her himself. How can he save her? After them, Roland, Hurry!"

The sleek stallion leapt forward, eating up the ground with its long smooth stride. Gaining on the two ahead, Greydon caught his breath as the gelding swerved from the open meadow and dodged into the growth of trees and brush surrounding it.

"Go on ahead, Geoff," he yelled as he cut towards the trees in pursuit. "He may swerve outward again."

Geoffrey looked back; his nod told the earl that he had understood.

On the gelding, Audacia was praying in earnest for her deliverance. The beast was far stronger than she had bargained for. Having taken the bit in its teeth, there was no way he could be halted by her.

The trees ranged dangerously close as the brute zigzagged among them. Greydon prayed he would reach her before she fell or was knocked from the saddle by a low-hanging branch.

The black's nose edged to the gelding's haunch. Greydon tensed his muscles as they slowly drew even. There would be but one chance to pull Audacia from the saddle, and if he missed his hold the danger that the gelding would shy and knock her against a tree or she would fall and be trampled was very real.

Daring not to look for fear of losing her hold, Audacia heard the pounding of a second set of hooves behind her and breathed her thanks with fear pounding in her throat.

"Count to three with me and let loose your hold on three," Greydon shouted as the animals pounded through the ever thickening undergrowth.

"One. Two. Three."

Completely trusting, Audacia forced her fingers to release their hold as the hard arm bit into her stomach and she was yanked free of the saddle. There was a rending sound as the skirt of her riding habit caught on the fork of her sidesaddle. Audacia's relief at being free of the gelding altered to dismay at seeing the greater part of her skirt flapping in the wind before her, frightening the steed to an ever greater speed. It turned to chagrin as she saw Geoffrey coming after the gelding from another angle.

The arm about her waist held her tightly against a firm, muscled body as the black was reined to a halt.

Letting the looped reins drop on the black's neck, Greydon drew Audacia to a sitting position across the front of his saddle.

"Greydon," she exclaimed, seeing her rescuer clearly for the first time.

With her straw bonnet hanging askew on its blue ribbons, black curls blown into disarray by the wind, and her face flushed with excitement, Audacia presented an almost irresistible lure to the earl. Even as he saw anger sparkle dangerously in her gray eyes, he had to rein hard on his desire to hold her close and kiss her full red lips, now parted slightly as she stared in surprise.

"Breeches would be more modest at the moment," he quipped, forcing his mind to another direction, "but not nearly as attractive as your lace."

Embarrassment was overwhelmed by indignation. Audacia spluttered incoherently, finally managing, "How dare you rescue me. You have ruined everything!"

A crooked smile came to the fore. "My dear Miss Aderly, your reactions never fail to astound me. I know of no other person in the kingdom who resents being kept from harm as you do." His look darkened as he thought of a second reason for her objection. "Geoff shall not take offense at seeing his loved one in my arms, nor any other man who pulls her from a bolting steed." His voice hardened and the gladness at seeing her safe was replaced by the old haunting hollowness. "It is my doing that he could not have rescued you. What was he to do? Drop his own reins to grab yours and be thrown himself?"

The depth of feeling behind Greydon's words shocked Audacia, threw her into a new confusion. "But you have spoilt it. If Geoffrey had shown Lady Lucille he could rescue me, then his confidence would have overflowed. She would have been able to assure him of her love in her admiring glances and all would have been set. Oh, I could just—You. Why is it always you?" Audacia's voice had risen with her temper.

"I ask the same," the earl said dryly. "Now will you call a halt to the hysterics and explain yourself? You speak as if you had planned for Geoff to rescue you."

"How else am I to help Lady Lucille accept the loss of his arm. She is as perverse in her thinking as you," she scolded, giving him a scorching glance.

"What an idiotic way to attempt a reconciliation. You

210

could have been seriously injured . . . killed." His voice rose in anger also.

"Oh, Roland . . . Audacia," Lady Lucille called out in relief as she spied them. Her look of comical alarm at the sight of Audacia's petticoats eased the tension. Pulling Daisy to a halt beside the pair she exclaimed, "Oh, lud, what has become of your skirt?"

"Here comes Geoffrey with it now. Little good that it will do me. I have no pins. How shall I return to Lady Darby?" The spoken thought staggered Audacia.

"Geoffrey is not holding the reins of his horse and yet it is obedient to his directions," Greydon noted aloud, surprised to see the squire mounted and leading Audacia's gelding.

"Have you never seen a circus, my lord?" Audacia asked sarcastically. "How do the trick riders command their horses and still have the use of their hands? Yes, they train them to respond to pressure cues. Geoffrey is not limited by himself but by others. He could and would have been able to rescue me," Audacia said as she looked straight at Lady Lucille, "if Lord Greydon had not interfered."

"Do not think Miss Aderly ungrateful, Lucille," the earl winked at his sister. "It is merely that I have not yet rescued her from the right circumstances. I am certain to find the proper one sooner or later."

"When did you save Audacia before this?" Lady Lucille appraised the two.

The squire saved both from answering with his timely arrival. "The mount you may not need," he said surveying Audacia still in Greydon's arms. "But this"—he nodded

211

at the blue swath of material draped across the gelding's saddle—"is definitely necessary."

"My lord," Audacia demanded, sternly glaring at Greydon.

"Yes?" he smiled innocently.

"Put me down—please," she said, restraining the desire to both laugh and cry as she looked into his ironic eyes.

In answer the earl released his hold immediately.

Audacia staggered as she landed on her feet with unexpected suddenness. Gritting her teeth she stamped to the gelding, pulled the skirt from the saddle and wrapped its fullness about her. "Does anyone have pins?" she asked, looking to Lady Lucille hopefully, only to find this lady staring at Geoffrey, a new appreciation written clearly over her features. At least all is not lost, Audacia thought gratefully.

"It will not be the height of fashion, Miss Aderly," Greydon said, dismounting, "but then we both know fashion is not your passion, if you will pardon the rhyme. This will do the task required."

Turning irritably to him, she watched as Greydon untied and unwrapped the stiff white cravat from about his neck. "If you will allow me," the earl said, reaching behind her and pulling the cravat over the skirt like a belt. "It is fortunate cravats have some length." He smiled as he tied the knot securely, his hands lingering momentarily.

Something in his eyes, in his face, drew and held Audacia. His teasing words passed unheard as his nearness sent a warmth coursing through her veins. She blanched and turned hurriedly from him, realizing how

212

close she had come to surrendering herself to his arms, to his lips in that moment.

"Audee, you missed a frightfully delicious supper. Are you certain I should not have Strowne bring something up for you?" Helene asked as she entered Audacia's room. "Is your headache better? What excitement! Squire Webster told us everything before he left this morn but Mother said I couldn't bother you till now," she said admiringly. "I should still be in hysterics if it were me. Are you certain it wasn't just as you planned?"

"No, it was very real, but I am fine," she assured her.

"But you are . . . so . . . wretched looking. Did the plan fail despite everything?"

"Time alone shall give the answer, but I have hopes that things are much improved between the two."

"Then why are you so sad? You look about to burst into tears."

Audacia briefly contemplated taking Helene into her confidence. How do you explain to one merely four and ten that you've suddenly discovered you are in love and despised by the one you love? she questioned herself and answered aloud, "I assure you I am fine."

"What a pleasure it is to hear those words," Lady Darby twittered coming into the room. "Then you shall be able to join us for a few moments. Patrick is beside himself with worry for you. A brief appearance on your part shall reassure the poor boy. Here, this gown will do," she said removing a lovely sprigged muslin in white and yellow from the wardrobe. "Let me assist you."

The determination on the viscountess's face brooked no escape.

"Miss Aderly, what a blessing! What a wonderful blessing to see you unharmed." Patrick Darby bowed over her hand and kissed it. "Please let me help you," he said taking her arm.

"I am quite recovered, Mr. Darby," she protested weakly, but certain that the viscountess was behind her, allowed him to lead her to the sofa in the small receiving salon. "It is kind of you to be concerned," Audacia added as she sat. Her eyes widened as Lady Darby's form disappeared behind the closing doors. "What—where is your mother going?" she asked in alarm.

"Please do not look so fearful, my dear Audacia," Patrick urged, capturing her hand in his.

"Mr. Darby, I must protest this unseemly behavior." She found her voice at last.

"My intentions are entirely honorable, Audacia. Surely you must have seen that you hold the highest place in my affections. Only say that you shall consent to be my wife."

"Mr. Darby," Audacia said, attempting to pull her hand from his.

"You have no choice, my dear one."

Managing to free her hand at last, she spoke as firmly as she could. "You must not speak to me in such an intimate manner. It should have been made clear to you after your last attempt to take advantage of me that I hold no feeling for you but contempt."

"That is unfortunate—for you," Patrick told her leaning insolently against the back of the sofa. "For I meant it when I said you had no choice."

"I bid you good eve," Audacia told him and walked toward the door.

"In the end you shall be mine," he sneered.

"There is no power on earth that could force me to accept you," she said without turning.

"You think so little of your brother then? And your father?"

"What have they to do with you?" she asked turning slowly, fear gripping her heart.

"I am not a vindictive man. If we wed I would simply ignore Daniel's debt."

"He owes you nothing." Remembrances of their conversation about gaming hells made the words a question.

"Daniel owes me over three thousand pounds, but why take my word? Speak to him. Then we shall meet once again. You shall find your affections altered, I am certain." He rose and walked to her. A chill went through Audacia as his hand brushed her cheek. "You are mine," Patrick told her with gloating confidence and sauntered from the room.

CHAPTER XXI

Pink rays streaked the horizon foretelling the sun's coming as the slight figure edged from the servants' door of No. 31 Mount Street. Glancing furtively about, the figure, clad in breeches, drew the light cloak tighter against the morning chill before dashing down the alley. Late-night revelers staggering homeward and early morning vendors taking their wares to market didn't give a second glance to the smudge-faced làd scooting past them.

The landlady at Viscount Hillern's was badly out of sorts at being roused at so uncomely an hour. "Mr. Aderly is asleep, lad. I'll not permit you to wake him," she scolded angrily at finding the unkempt figure at her door.

"I was told to deliver this letter only to him, ma'am," the lad argued. "Let me into his chambers and I'll not stir till he wakes."

"And steal everything of value," she scoffed. "Who did you say the letter is from?"

"His lordship, the Earl of Greydon."

"Loo, these bluebloods," the woman complained. "Follow me. Mr. Aderly can take his ire out on you and his lordship."

At the first knock, the door opened.

"Why Mr. Aderly," the landlady said in surprise, "you're about." Ah, well, no doubt just returned, she told herself. "This lad has a letter from Lord Greydon. Give it to him, lad," she prodded him forward.

"I'm to give it to Mr. Aderly . . . with him bein' alone. And wait his answer," the boy said resisting her urging.

Throwing her hands up in disgust, the landlady bid Daniel a good morn and departed.

"Where is the letter?" Daniel demanded nervously. "I have little time to waste. Come, lad, I'm about to depart."

"At this hour? Is that why Geoffrey has been unable to find you?"

"Audee . . . what on earth?" Daniel's eyes widened in amazement. "Did anyone see you come here? My God! What possessed you to dress so?"

"I had to speak with you," she answered, pulling the cap from her head and taking a chair in the sitting room. "Are we alone?"

"Yes, I don't know where Hillern is. He and Darby did not return with me."

Audacia paled beneath the dirty smears. "Were you gambling?" she asked in hushed tones.

He nodded numbly and sank into a chair beside her. "I don't know what I'm to do, Audee. Darby holds notes against me for over five thousand pounds."

"Five thousand pounds! That's a fortune. But how can he . . . ?" Fear tightened its cold hand about her heart.

217

"Surely you did not—" Audacia reached out and covered his hand with hers.

Remorse hung over him.

"It is true, then," came from her in sentencing tones. "How long before you must pay?"

Shrugging, Daniel looked up guiltily. "Debts of honor must be met immediately." His eyes fell from hers and he chewed his lip nervously. "But Darby says he may forgive the debt. He says"—a furtive glance went to his sister—"if I were 'family' there would be no need to pay."

"Family" rang in Audacia's mind. No wonder Patrick was so bold. "Have you spoken with Father?" she asked hollowly.

"How can I, Audee? You know all his income other than what goes for my schooling and allowance is put into his machines." Daniel dropped his head sorrowfully into his hands. "I don't know what to do, Audee," he moaned.

"Could Father pay the sum? Do you know?"

"Not without selling everything. Even that may not be sufficient. Could you not learn to care for Patrick even a little?" The revulsion on Audacia's face struck his last hope. "I have brought us all to ruin," Daniel sobbed dryly.

Audacia knelt on the floor before her brother and wrapped her arms about him. "There must be some way out of this," she told him. "We shall find it."

"There is ruin for you no matter which way I turn." He looked at her, guilt darkening his face with tinges of despair. "What a fool I have been."

"Could not Geoffrey help?" She grasped at a fleeting straw.

"He has little reason to, and most of his funds are tied up in improvements," Daniel returned, shaking his head.

218

"Let us see to some breakfast. Then we shall be able to think more clearly," Audacia told him, rising to her feet. "Go, order some brought here."

"But it is far too early. Won't Lady Darby be in whoops at finding you gone?"

"She won't think to check my room till noon," she dismissed the thought. "I'm famished. Hurry now."

"What are we to do, Audee?" Daniel asked as they finished their meal. "I cannot face Father. I would rather die."

"Don't speak such nonsense," Audacia returned sharply, frightened by his tone and look as well as by the words.

"Daniel," Squire Webster's voice sounded with his knock. "Daniel, we hear you talking. Let Lord Greydon and myself enter."

"They must not see me," Audacia said, rising hurriedly.

"My room. There." He pointed. "Hurry." Daniel rose and walked to the door. "Come in," he greeted his guests.

"We find you at last," Geoffrey greeted him with a critical eye. "I had begun to fear your sister's concern was well warranted. Word has it that your losses have been heavy. Do not fear to speak before Roland." The squire waved a hand at his friend. "We both wish to help you if it is needed."

"I am no green youth whose hand needs to be held." Daniel straightened himself stiffly.

"We mean no offense," Greydon said, stepping forward, "but Darby may have led you deeper than you can safely tread. But perhaps such matters should be discussed elsewhere. Your guest . . ." he nodded questioningly at the dishes for two upon the table.

"A friend—a friend from school," Daniel stuttered. "We are to join some others at Lord's cricket ground," he uttered, using the first thing he thought of as excuse.

"So early in the morn?" Geoffrey questioned.

"It is a practice match."

"And we are late in going," Audacia strode from the bedchamber dressed in one of Daniel's suits. "We had better go, Aderly," she added, hoping her altered voice was deep enough to pass as a young man's.

"Mr. Aderly." The landlady knocked upon the door and entered. "Would you be wishing tea brought for the gentlemen?" Her keen eye ended on Audacia.

"That will not be necessary, Mrs. Harris," Daniel said, going to her side. "We are just now departing."

"If you are certain . . ."

"Most certain." He took her elbow and turned her to the corridor. "Thank you," he spoke nervously and smiled as he closed the door.

"There is nothing to fear Squire Webster, Lord Greydon. I thank you for your offer but you must excuse me now." Daniel opened the door to find Mrs. Harris lingering.

"Good day, Mr. Aderly." Greydon nodded and motioned Geoffrey to follow him as he stepped towards the door.

"Come to me if you have need for anything," the squire told Daniel. Giving a last curious glance at Daniel's friend, he followed Roland from the room.

With the pair safely gone, Daniel closed the door. "You must leave. Hillern could return at any time. It would be ghastly if you were discovered here . . . dressed like that."

220

"I think I make a rather handsome lad," Audacia returned saucily.

"Oh, Audee, what have I done to you?" he moaned.

Her spirit refused to sag with his. "We are not at ends yet."

Daniel snorted. "I have not even enough to lend you for a hansom."

"Do not fret about it. I want you to promise me you will go to Father today. You needn't tell him the whole of the matter, but see him," she urged.

"I don't know, Audee."

"You must." She kissed his cheek lightly. "Call on me this eve. I will let you know what I have learned. A solution can be found. I know it," Audacia said to bolster his spirits.

"Dear sister, if I had but listened to you from the first."

"No more of that," she ordered. "Go to Father. I'll await you this eve." With a reassuring hug, she left him. On the street she obtained a hansom and ordered it to the back entrance of the Mount Street residence.

"Are you going to follow her?" Geoffrey asked as the two men watched Audacia climb into the hansom.

"Till she's safely at Darby's," Greydon bit out. "That hoyden, what has she taken into her head this time? Doesn't she realize the consequences if she is discovered gadding about dressed as a man . . . and in a bachelor's quarters no less."

"Audacia is not foolish. It must have been a matter of great import to have caused her to dare this. Have you been able to learn just how much Daniel owes?"

"Over three thousand pounds at last reckoning. A mas-

221

sive sum for one with his small expectations. Or do I misjudge Aderly's holdings?"

"Rather not, I think." Geoffrey shook his head. "You say those you spoke with think Darby led the lad deliberately to lose such sums? The cur. I'm of a mind that he should be dealt with."

"First let us learn what he means to gain. Everything points to his wishing to force Audacia to wed him but for the fact it makes no sense. He needs an heiress. Her dowry would hardly keep the man for two days." Greydon's visage hardened. "Mr. Darby shall not be as fortunate as when we last met."

"So it was you who dealt him the facer," Geoffrey assessed his suddenly uncomfortable friend. "You take an uncommon interest in Audacia for one who has been given a deathly chill and nearly impaled to death by the lady," he noted casually.

"You object?" came the surprising question.

"Why, no. Not at all. Why should *I* object? It is your life you chance," the squire said and chuckled dryly.

Greydon threw him a withering look, then urged his whites after the hansom.

"Daniel probably forgot," Helene tried to calm Audacia as the latter paced about the salon. "You know how brothers can be."

"He promised he would come. What if something dreadful has happened?" Audacia wrung her hands.

"No harm can come to him with Patrick watching over him," Lady Darby said as she stitched on her needlepoint.

Audacia looked more and more worried. The long case clock chimed, causing her to start.

"You have worked yourself into a fever, Audacia," the viscountess looked up from her work. "See Helene to bed. I shall call you if your brother comes."

Helene took Audacia's reluctant hand and led the way upstairs.

"Why are you so worried, Audee?" she asked as she climbed into bed.

Straightening the light covers, Audacia smiled sadly and sat on the bedside. "I can find no solution to another problem. The only answers are distressingly dreadful," she sighed.

"We needn't dress like lads if that is what troubles you so," Helene offered.

"It is not that." Audacia shook her head. "I wish it were."

"Can you not tell me what then?"

"It—it involves a friend—a friend from Warwickshire. Daniel was telling me of her troubles. I so wish I could find a solution for her. You see, this friend, Beth, has a brother much like Daniel and he went to London and lost a horrible sum of money gambling. One of his friends signed the notes and Beth's brother thought he had nothing to fear, but now the friend says Beth must marry him or he will call the debts due. If he does this, her family loses everything."

"That is horrible!" Helene exclaimed. "Is there no one to lend the sum?"

"None."

"Would it be so terrible for your friend to marry this man? Mother has oft said how her parents arranged for her to wed Father long before they met."

Audacia studied her hands closely. "At one time it

would not have been so difficult . . . but—but Beth has discovered she is in love with another."

"Will he not aid her?" the young girl asked brightly, seeing the simple answer.

"Oh . . . Beth would not dare to speak to him of it. She believes he—knows he does not return her affection." Her voice shook and she fought back threatening tears.

"Then he is not worthy," Helene told her with youthfully easy dismissal.

"But he is," broke from Audacia and she ran from the room.

"Mother dear." Darby kissed the cheek the viscountess turned to him. "How are you this eve? I had hoped to find Audacia with you," he said looking about the salon. "Is it not early for her to have retired?"

"She has not. Trotter, call Miss Audacia to return to the salon," the viscountess ordered. "She is in Miss Helene's room."

"Do not tell her I have arrived," Darby added.

The butler gone, Lady Darby gave her son a deep frown. "I expected to be able to send an announcement to the *Gazette* today, and now you cannot count on her presence if she knows you are here?"

"Audacia is not as willing as one might wish," Patrick answered lightly. "Shyness on her part, no doubt."

"Have you failed with her? You know what that would mean to us? You must not. There has to be some way to persuade the chit," Lady Darby said desperately. "I was so hoping . . ."

"Do not fear, Mother. She will consent."

"There is nothing but ruin and disgrace if you fail.

224

Already the duns are calling. You have lived far beyond our means, and without a betrothal announcement soon, they shall cut off all credit. I am desperate, Patrick. You must realize how perilous our position is."

"You have told me that many times, Mother. Be assured I shall succeed. You shall be able to announce our betrothal or . . . marriage," he said as he adjusted his cravat jauntily, "on the morrow."

The viscountess blanched slightly. "Marriage? You are not using force to—" Her words ended abruptly.

"You wished to see me, my lady?" Audacia halted as she saw Patrick to one side. "I wish to retire, my lady, a terrible headache plagues me," she added and backed a step toward the door.

"Nonsense, my dear. Patrick is just the one to soothe your nerves. It is quite natural for you to be maidenly demure, but put your fears aside." Lady Darby rose. "I shall leave you two alone for just a few moments, now," she gushed expectantly as she walked past her.

"My dear Audacia, would it not be more proper to kiss your betrothed rather than to glare at him so?" Patrick smirked.

"You are not my betrothed and never shall be," she returned in as firm a voice as she could muster.

"Have you not seen Daniel?"

"We must have time. All will be repaid," Audacia told him. "You cannot mean to take all my father has."

"Only if you refuse me," he stated coldly. "Why resist? You know you cannot escape."

"I shall never consent, never." Her nails dug into her palms as she clenched her fists. "My father will not permit this to happen."

"Are you truly so simple-minded, Audacia? I thought better of you. Your father will have no choice when he learns all."

"I don't care. I shall never marry you. Never."

"We shall speak about it on the morrow, when you have conquered your hysteria. Go now." He waved irritably.

Refusing to give into the panic that threatened, Audacia glared at him and walked calmly from the room.

"Well?" Lady Darby questioned upon reentering. "Did she consent?"

"I shall return in the morn. The matter will be resolved then. You will aid me by not being present."

"You must persuade her." The viscountess clutched her son's arm. "All is lost if you do not."

CHAPTER XXII

Dark circles beneath Audacia's eyes bespoke her sleepless, tormented night. All through the dark hours she had wrestled with her choices, none of which was satisfactory in any way. The thought of wedding Darby repulsed her so, she could not bear to consider it; the losses of her home and the ruination of her father and brother were hardly more appealing. About halfway through the night she had suddenly thought to seek Lord Greydon's help as Helene had suggested, but this, too, seemed an impossible step.

The lack of sleep and the strain of her troubles caused Audacia to quail momentarily as Patrick Darby hurried into the breakfast room. What small appetite she had fled.

"Audacia, how fortunate you are about. Fetch your bonnet and pelisse. You must come with me at once," he urged excitedly.

"There is no reason for—"

"It is Daniel. He is asking for you."

227

"Oh, Lord no," she breathed, stricken. "He has not harmed himself?"

Darby nodded. "Daniel has shot himself. I blame myself," he said bowing his head. "Please hurry. You must see him before it is too—"

"Return to your carriage," Audacia told him, cutting off his words. "I shall join you immediately."

"Where are you racing to?" Helene followed as Audacia ran through the upper floor's corridor to her room.

"Daniel shot himself," the other returned, jabbing her bonnet atop her curls and fumbling with the ties. "Patrick is taking me to him now." She took the young girl's hand in hers. "Pray for him, Helene. He must live."

"I shall," she answered, shaken by the news. She followed Audacia down the steps and out the door.

Darby scowled and ordered his sister to return indoors as he handed Audacia into the closed carriage.

How odd, thought Helene, for him to have a closed carriage and four. Surely a hansom would have been faster? Shrugging, she dismissed the thought, her concern turning to Audacia and the news of her brother.

"Miss Helene, have you seen Miss Audacia," the abigail asked after having gone through the house in search of her charge.

"Have you not heard the news, Miss Strowne?" Helene asked. "But then I suppose there was not time to tell everyone. I had thought we would have gotten word by now," she added as the long case clock struck eleven. "It has been at least an hour since they left."

"Miss, begin again. You make no sense," Miss Bea admonished.

"Patrick came for Audee. Daniel has shot himself."

The abigail turned chalk-white and began to waver to and fro. She made her way to a chair and sat. "Does he still live?"

"I believe so. Patrick wouldn't have fetched Audee in such a great rush if he were dead, would he?"

"I suppose not." Miss Bea fanned herself. "Oh, poor Sir Aderly. This is terrible. Why would the lad do such a thing? I must go to him at once. Where did this happen?"

Helene shrugged. "So little was said," she explained uneasily, recalling what she had overheard Patrick tell Trotter.

Wringing her hands, the abigail rose. "I must know how he is. Lady Darby will know what to—"

"Mother left before Patrick came," Helene interrupted her.

"Then I shall go to Sir Aderly's rooms. Surely they would have taken the lad there."

"I shall go with you," Helene informed her and was surprised to find Miss Bea too upset to think to refuse her.

In moments they were in the hansom Trotter procured for them and were on their way to Pultney's.

"Miss Strowne," a shocked Ballin greeted the abigail when he opened the door to her knock. "This is a most unexpected . . . and pleasant surprise. But what brings you here alone?" he winked teasingly.

"Please Mr. Ballin. How can you at a time like this?" she said tremulously. "Where have they taken the poor boy?"

"I am sorry, Miss Bea, I don't understand." He studied her quizzically. "Sir Aderly is meeting with Richard

Trevithick about his attempts with a steam threshing machine and isn't to return till this eve."

"You mean he has not heard? Oh, lud. What are we to do?" she clucked anxiously.

"Heard what? Here. Come, take a seat. You look frightfully pale, Bea." Ballin took her arm and guided her to a chair.

"It is Daniel," the abigail told him, sitting heavily. "He has . . . shot himself," she sobbed, her tears falling freely.

"Let me get you some brandy," Ballin muttered. Pouring two large draughts, he quaffed one and took the other to Bea. "Drink this," he urged, pressing it into her hands. "You will feel better for it."

One sip assured her it was to be swallowed in one gulp. The brandy burned a warm path, reviving her quickly. "What are we to do, Mr. Ballin? He could be dying . . . or . . . dead." Miss Bea sobbed anew.

"Calm yourself, woman." The valet's hard tone straightened her. "Have you no pride? There'll be time enough for blubbering after the fact. Did ye come here alone?" he asked as he struggled into his jacket and grabbed his hat.

"Miss Darby awaits me in the lobby," she sniffed in answer.

"Let us get her in tow and find Sir Aderly," Ballin told her, taking her arm and aiding her to rise. "That is more like the Miss Strowne I know," he praised her as she rose and strode forward purposefully.

"Sir Aderly and Mr. Trevithick left some time ago and the butler doesn't know their direction," Ballin told Miss Bea as he climbed back into the hansom, crowded with

Helene squeezed between them. "We shall go on to Squire Webster and see what he recommends," he told them and gave the address to the driver.

"Oh, you are so masterful," Miss Bea sighed. "I would never have known what to do."

"You would have managed, Bea," he said, reaching across Helene to pat her hand.

She blushed and bit her lip. "That is most kind of you."

Helene glanced from one to the other, then sighed in disgust. Was everyone in the world, even the servants, affected by "love"? "Mr. Aderly may have died by the time we find him," she pointed out because of her annoyance.

Starting guiltily, Miss Bea withdrew her hand.

Glaring at Helene, Ballin drew his hand back. "We shall hope for better," he told the abigail stoutly and was rewarded by a shy smile.

"The squire wants you both to come in and tell him what you know." Ballin opened the hansom cab's door and motioned for the two to come out. "He has ordered the earl's landau. Go in while I take care of the cab," he instructed and turned to the driver.

"You are certain Audacia said Daniel had shot himself?" Geoffrey asked a second time.

"How many times must I say it," Helene objected to the questioning.

"But I spoke with Daniel just an hour past," the squire told the three anxious figures before him.

"That is impossible," Miss Bea declared. "Helene said Mr. Darby came for Audacia near ten this morn."

"There is some foul work afoot here. Let us go find Lord

Greydon. I know he will be interested. Come, the landau should be awaiting us. I believe we shall find him at his mother's. He was to call upon his sister on my behalf," he half frowned, one concern outweighing another at the moment, as he strode past the three.

"But why would Mr. Darby tell Miss Audacia her brother was dying when he wasn't?" Miss Bea asked, turning to Ballin.

"Not all men are honorable, pardon my words, miss." He bowed to Helene. "I fear Miss Audacia may have been abducted."

The abigail raised her hand to her mouth in fright. "Oh, my. Oh, dear," she clucked.

"Do not fear." Ballin took her hand. "The squire and I shall see that she is unharmed."

"With you to rely upon, Mr. Ballin, I trust for only the best results," Miss Bea told him, returning his grip. "Your worth has been hidden from me too long."

Ballin reddened even as his chest swelled. "I pray I am worthy of such praise," he replied, "and high it is comin' from the like o' ye." Beneath Miss Bea's doting look he dared not voice his assessment of Audacia's fate.

"Will you two come or not?" Helene called impatiently to them from the door.

Holding hands, the pair followed her hurriedly.

"But this is ghastly," Lady Lucille said when Miss Bea and Helene had finished their tale. "What can he mean to do, Roland?" She turned to her brother and was taken aback by the utter grimness of his expression.

"I know not what his intent is, but her reputation will

be ruined if word of this gets abroad," the earl bit out. "What do you make of it, Geoff?"

"If only we could make some sense of why," the squire returned. "It could give us some clue to his direction. Did Audacia ever speak about Darby?" he asked Lady Lucille.

"Never," she answered simply. "You must do something."

Taking her hand, Geoffrey gave it a reassuring squeeze. "We'll take some action." Her hand still in his, he turned to Greydon.

"But what, Geoff?" the earl asked, his inability to go to Audacia's aid contorting his features.

"I—I think I could . . . tell you why," a quiet voice boomed in the silence.

All eyes turned to Helene.

"Once . . . some time ago, I heard Mother and Patrick talking. They were—were speaking about Audacia and that Patrick must marry her."

"Did you hear why?" Geoffrey asked.

"Oh, yes. Mother said Sir Aderly had revealed that Audacia had a dowry—a legacy from her mother's family. And although there was no amount mentioned, Mother was certain it would be large enough to solve all our problems."

Greydon looked to Geoffrey to assess the truth of it.

"It could be so. I have no way of knowing. Miss Bea?"

She shook her head. "I can't imagine there being much there. Lady Aderly's family was well-to-do but it all went to the Aderly heir."

"So we know he means to wed her, but that is no help." Greydon threw up his hands in disgust.

"I know where Patrick means to take Audee," Helene added, guiltily.

"Oh, please tell us all," Lady Lucille implored, taking the young girl's hands.

Helene began haltingly, her voice growing stronger as she went on. "He means to take her to Chatham. I—I heard him tell Trotter a joke about a preacher there willing to marry anyone for a price, even unwilling women," she ended, her head hanging low. "He always tried to get the best of poor Trotter." She looked at the five staring at her. "I really did believe what he told Audacia about her brother."

"I'll see to the high-perch phaeton and my fastest four," Greydon told Geoffrey as he ran from the room.

"I'll go with you," Lady Lucille said, also galvanized into action as she headed to collect her bonnet and traveling cloak. "Audacia may have need of me."

"I did right, didn't I, squire?" Helene asked, a small tear running down her cheek. "I couldn't let Patrick hurt Audee, could I?"

"You did the only thing you could, Helene," Geoffrey told her, drawing her into a one-armed hug. "Life often gives us difficult choices," he told her. "You only did what had to be done. Do not worry. All will be well."

She wiped her eyes with the back of her hand. "Last eve Audee told me it was a friend from Warwickshire who was being made to marry . . . but she meant herself," she said aloud as she realized the truth of Audacia's tale. "She meant she could not marry Patrick because she loved someone else. That cannot be you, squire, but who? Audee believes he despises her, whoever it is. Do you know who it could be?"

Geoffrey didn't answer, for Greydon had returned and overheard Helene's words.

Joy and deep regret lay mixed upon the earl's features. "We must not tarry," he swore and turned on heel, a running stride carrying him out of sight.

"Ballin," Geoffrey ordered, motioning the valet to walk with him as he spoke. "Say nothing of this to Sir Aderly . . . nor to anyone else, including the Darbys. If God wills it we shall return this eve with Audacia, or send word as to her fate. Plead ignorance, offer no explanations. Thus whatever we put forth will not be contradicted. Understood?"

"Aye, squire. You can rely on Miss Bea and myself."

"Good man," Geoffrey said, clapping him on the shoulder.

"Await me," Lady Lucille called, running toward them.

Taking her hand as she came abreast, Geoffrey gave her a bolstering smile before they ran after Greydon.

CHAPTER XXIII

Sitting ramrod straight on her side of the enclosed coach, Audacia continued to add to her list of impolite adjectives that she felt suited Patrick Darby. It had not taken long after she entered the coach to learn his true intent. The relief of knowing that Daniel was unharmed was quickly replaced by anger, which added to the general upheaval of her emotions.

Lounging in the opposite corner, Darby gazed at Audacia with the fascination of a viper. "The journey could be far more comfortable if you relaxed; and far more pleasant for us both if you abandoned your false dignity," he told her lazily. "Still not speaking, eh?" Patrick noted when he got no response. "Have it your way now, my dear, but remember that when we arrive in Chatham I shall have mine."

"No cleric will do as you say," Audacia bit out angrily, breaking her silence.

236

Patrick patted his jacket. "With this special license I have no fears. Shouldn't you be bloody glad he shall wed us?" Darby leaned forward and ran his finger along the curve of her cheek. "After this night you would beg me to marry you." His finger trailed down her throat towards the low neckline of her morning gown.

Shuddering, Audacia pushed his hand away.

Darby chuckled maliciously as he leaned back against the cushions.

A chill ran through Audacia at his look.

Geoffrey mounted the landau. "A coach and four like Helene described passed this way a little under two hours past," he told the waiting pair.

"We'll never catch them in time," Lady Lucille said dismally.

"If he has touched her I will kill him," Greydon bit out as he eased his four back to the main road and urged them to top speed. "I'll make her a widow if she is a bride when we arrive."

Lady Lucille glanced at Geoffrey. Never had she heard her brother speak so darkly, and in her fear she turned instinctively to the squire.

He shook his head and squeezed her hand tightly. They bowed their heads in mutual prayer.

Farther away from London the traffic lessened into an occasional horseman or coach. Greydon halted at the Lion's Paw and exchanged his lathered, winded teams for two fresh pair. In minutes the landau was bowling along, a trail of dust marking its progress, while three pair of eyes strained ahead for the miracle of the sight of the coach they pursued.

237

Many miles before them the coach Darby and Audacia rode in threw both from their seats as it bounced heavily through one, then two more, deep ruts. After the third it came to a splintering halt. Darby tumbled cursing from the coach.

Benumbed by the spirits he'd been nipping, the coachman ignored Darby as he climbed laboriously down from the box. Assessing the damage, he muttered, "Broken spokes." Deliberate steps took him to the teams and he began unhitching the first pair.

Darby, who had continued his haranguing all the while, was inflamed by the coachman's total disregard. Reaching out, he spun the man around and threw a light punch into his face.

"Whach ye doin' thet fer?" The man focused bleary eyes on his attacker.

"What do you mean to do about that wheel?" Patrick blustered angrily. "I must get to Chatham before dusk."

"Well, thet 'er wheel ain't goin' ta take ye."

"I know that. What are you going to do about it?"

"Why, ride ahead to the next inn and fetch a wheel back." The coachman shook his head at the man's ignorance. His amiable air began to turn sour with Darby's continued scolding.

"Hurry now, you fool. I shall double your fee if you manage to return in good time. What is wrong with you?" he quibbled as the coachman crawled atop one of the wide-backed pair. "Hurry, you dolt," Patrick called after him as he swayed perilously close to falling off the awkwardly trotting coach horse. Its partner followed unwillingly.

"Double me fee, the chap says. His likes usually ferget

ta pay a'tall. Think his lordship could use a lesson. Wouldn't hurt 'im ta wait a few hours more than need be." The coachman glanced back at the pompous, strutting buck and burst into a deep laugh. "Do 'im good," he said aloud and enjoyed the thought of his justice all the way to the inn.

Hearing Darby's strident tones and insulting words, Audacia momentarily put aside her own distress. "That is no way to speak to an honest workman," she reprimanded Patrick as she stepped down from the coach.

"That drunken dolt? What does he know of honest work?" he scoffed.

"Far more than you ever will," Audacia snapped, her temper barely under control after the day's events.

"Get back inside the coach. I'll not have you trying to steal away," Darby told her querulously, the accident shaking his confidence for the first time.

"Where am I to run in these," she scoffed, raising her skirts to show the satin slippers she had neglected to change from in her rush to reach Daniel. "And the horses must be put in the shade," she protested. "They could bolt and hurt themselves if they remain hitched to the coach."

"Let them. Get inside, I say."

"I don't care to be in a coach dragged along by panicked horses," she shot back and strode towards the team. Her steps changed to a limping tiptoeing as the clods and sharp-edged ruts of the rough road bruised her feet, inadequately protected by the satin slippers.

"Hardly likely you can go far," Darby noted, watching her, and laughed. "Even when my plans are momentarily snared by an accident such as this, fortune still watches over me," he boasted. Pulling a silver flask from his jacket, he tipped it up and drank deeply.

Audacia ignored him, a false calm coming over her as she had the physical relief of action in unhitching the team. She led them to a nearby tree and tied them securely.

"A drink, my dearest?" Patrick invited her, holding the flask out as he followed.

A look of contempt was flashed in answer.

Walking up to her, Darby grabbed Audacia's arm and pulled her roughly to another tree not far from the team. "Sit," he ordered, pushing her to the ground. He sat heavily and leaned against the tree. After a disgruntled grimace at the coach he drank deeply.

Straightening herself, Audacia rubbed her bruised feet and threw a furtive glance at Patrick. Fear, anger, then repugnance had been the ruling emotions thus far, but fear began to rise as she saw Darby fling the empty flask aside. Fear grew as he rose and stalked to the coach and removed a bottle of port. Patrick sober was one matter; drunk, another entirely. Her eyes sought the stretch of road they had traveled. Someone, anyone, she prayed in a growing desperation, come—come and help me.

An hour passed and Darby got a second bottle of port from the coach's boot. This he emptied as he had the flask and the first bottle. His face had become flushed, his motions loose. His mood began to shift from sullen to malicious. "Thought you'd not marry me, eh?" He lurched to his feet and weaved to where Audacia sat. "You're not so proud now, my pretty." He grabbed her and pulled her to her feet. "A kiss for your intended," he demanded, yanking her against him. Neither he nor Audacia saw the bobbing phaeton approaching at a breakneck pace as they struggled.

Bearing down on the stricken coach at a speed that bore no respect for the limbs of the animals pulling it or the men atop it, the phaeton was well past Audacia and Darby before Greydon could rein the sweating teams to a halt. Geoffrey leapt down as they passed the grappling pair, staggered as he hit the ground, regained his footing, and took long, running strides toward them.

Twisting about in her seat, Lady Lucille watched as the squire reached the pair. Darby still held onto Audacia. Geoffrey's arm wrenched one of Darby's hands from her and a straight-legged kick to Darby's stomach doubled him over in pain. The squire's well-muscled arm sent a fist smashing into his jaw and Darby lurched backward. He began to step toward his assailant uncertainly when a second blow sent him sprawling to the ground, unconscious.

Exultant, Lady Lucille jumped to the ground and ran towards them: Geoffrey in shock at his success and Audacia barely able to manage a smile, the danger she had just escaped still too real.

The squire recovered from his surprise in time to steady Audacia, who had begun trembling. Lady Lucille enveloped them both in a joyous hug.

Greydon, a deep scowl on his face, watched the scene as he turned the teams about on the road. So much for rescuing Audacia and erasing all her misconceptions, he thought darkly.

In the wild enthusiasm of the moment, Geoffrey found Lady Lucille's arms about him and was suddenly kissing her soundly. Realizing this, he drew back totally alarmed, positive he had ruined any chance he might have had. But before him, gazing in dazzling happiness, Lady Lucille reached up and drew his lips slowly to hers once again.

Audacia, who had stepped back from the pair, felt her spirit rise with their happiness. Success with their cause was certain. After a glance to assess Darby's state, she walked to the broken-down coach. Finding herself still shaking, she laid a hand on the wheel to steady herself.

"Don't you think you went rather far in your scheming to bring them to their senses?" Greydon's angry voice startled her.

"Far?" Audacia turned to him in outrage. Her emotions had been too stretched, had swung too violently and too far to deal with this man sensibly. "Far!" she spluttered again, hopelessly torn between anger and the overwhelming desire to rush into his arms.

"Did you teach Geoff how to manage that as well?" Greydon asked, directing his gaze back to the ardently embracing pair.

Red flared to her cheeks.

"Mayhaps you have a mind to teach me, also?" the earl continued, half serious, half teasing as his mind groped for words that would not come beneath Audacia's strange, intense gaze.

"Why Geoffrey values you as a friend is beyond understanding," she retorted, stoking her anger to prevent her spirit from failing beneath his impassive stare.

"Your gratitude overwhelms me once more, Miss Aderly. I have ruined my best bloods to reach you before Darby—in time," he amended his words as she blanched.

"I believe you are actually jealous of Geoffrey. Jealous that it was he who leveled Darby," she exclaimed indignantly, realizing part of Greydon's emotions with sudden clarity. "Haven't you kept him a cripple in your mind long enough?"

"His lacking is of my making. You needn't remind me of that. I live with it daily." The earl admitted aloud for the first time the guilt that had ridden him since Portugal. "Look at him. Why do you pretend he has not lost the arm?!"

"Yes, *look* at him," Audacia repeated with equal force. "Does he look different from any other man?" Her voice softened and she stepped forward, laying a hand upon Greydon's taut arm. This battle was for him and for herself as well as for Geoffrey. "You have both your arms, but—"

"God, don't you think I know that." He whirled away from her touch. "I have lived with this from the moment it was done. If I could have I would have torn my own arm off." The earl's eyes flared wide and his breath came in heavy gasps.

"You have no right to say such things," Audacia told him, her edge of calm almost shattered by the day's rolling turmoil, by the power of the emotions she felt flowing from the tortured man before her.

"He took a ball meant for *me*. Can't you understand that? It should have been my arm, not Geoff's." A tear rolled down Greydon's face.

"If it had been meant to be, it would have been your arm. Are you so buried beneath your self-pity that you cannot see that? Many men lost limbs in the wars and many did not. Thank God for those that were spared. Free the ones who were not from your self-pity." She flung aside what little caution, what little control remained.

"Enough." Greydon's voice seared her. "What can you know—"

"What? I know it is time regret, useless regret, was over and done with," Audacia implored. "When did you last look at Geoffrey and see *him*, not his missing arm? He has faced it, acknowledged it gone. Now you must," she pleaded. "Instead of pitying him, realize it is yourself you pity. You took an arm, but gave him life. Look, is he cursing you for it?"

Greydon's eyes swung about and met Geoffrey's as he and Lucille approached, his arm about her. For the first time the earl realized what it was in his friend's look that had puzzled him since he had been to Warwickshire. It was pity for him, for he who still had both arms.

"Take your guilt and purge it by action." The earl heard Audacia's voice as if it came from afar. "Have you not seen the streets of London filled with the butchered men of the wars? Find a use for their lives. Give them a purpose," she challenged, "and you may find the vindication for your life that you seek." Her words echoed hollowly as she saw his look harden, his eyes refuse to meet hers.

"Geoff, take them, take them both in the phaeton and return to London as quickly as you can," Greydon rasped, ignoring Audacia's pleading stance before him. "That's an order, Lieutenant." His voice cracked. His eyes blazed angrily at Audacia for a scant condemning second. "Our mission will not be ended until there is no chance of rumor left. I'll remain with Darby and return when his coach is repaired. Take her." He grabbed Audacia's arm and pushed her forward.

Lady Lucille darted to the frozen figure, took her arm, and led her to the phaeton.

With an angry shake of his head, Greydon dismissed any words Geoffrey would have said as he paused before him.

Mutely the squire gripped the earl's shoulder, giving silent comfort, then walked on.

After helping Audacia to the phaeton's seat, Lady Lucille scrambled up herself and picked up the reins. The squire joined the women, climbing onto the seat.

"Can you manage four?" Lady Lucille asked.

"If you place the reins for me," he answered, spreading his fingers before her. "They should be jaded enough to cause no trouble, but it will not be easy. One is enough for me to handle. I cannot do everything," Geoffrey told her, his eyes speaking of far more than the teams before them.

"It will be an honor to help you . . . always, if you will allow me to," she told him.

Gently they kissed, exchanging their lifelong pledge to one another. Both heard the low, dry sob break from Audacia and turned to her.

"I—I am so—so happy for you." She made a valiant attempt to smile but failed. "So happy" was repeated as she looked back to Greydon, who turned from her.

Geoffrey flicked the reins, thankful that Greydon had turned the teams about. As they put their weight to the harness, Lady Lucille gripped Audacia's hand. When they rounded the first bend in the road, she said with an understanding born of her own experience, "He cannot see you now," and opened her arms as Audacia turned to her, disconsolate tears streaming.

CHAPTER XXIV

A bright August sun cast the short shadows of midday as Audacia entered the modest rose-red Keuper stone house. She spied the letters upon the table in the entryway immediately and grabbed them hungrily. A soft, sorrowful sigh escaped as she turned them over and saw Lady Lucille's neat hand upon one and Daniel's heavy scrawl upon the other. Walking toward her father's workshop, Audacia broke the seal on Lucille's missive and read.

"Will the squire and his bride be coming home soon?" Sir Maurice asked, looking up from his work as his daughter walked slowly into the workshop, her head deep in the letter.

"Yes, they are to return in less than a week if I read this correctly."

"It will be good for you to have someone to visit," Sir Aderly said, his eyes returning to his work but his concern remaining with his thin, sad-eyed daughter.

"Yes," she returned vaguely. "Lucille mentions here that they stopped in Reading to visit Helene at the school Lord Grey—at the school she was sent to. Says they found her quite happy and looking forward to her proposed visit here next month." She read along silently then quickly folded it and asked, "How does the work progress?"

"Slowly as usual. Ballin should be returning soon with the gear I ordered made in London. I have great hope it will be a step forward."

"You will succeed, Father, I am certain."

"I wish I were that positive," Sir Aderly said tightening a bolt. Father and daughter looked at each other, their thoughts shared; the success of the harvesting machine had become of utmost importance with Lord Greydon's purchase of partial rights in it for over £5,000. The knowledge of their debt weighed heavily, if for different reasons, on both.

"What did Daniel write?" Sir Aderly asked.

Breaking the seal on the second letter, Audacia read hurriedly. "He says he is learning much from Mr. Adams and is looking forward to returning to school this fall. The choice of becoming a solicitor evidently has proven well founded with him," she noted happily.

"Good. Good," her father sighed. "His lesson was hard but he has matured because of it. It was good of Lord Greydon to tell me what the lad wished to do." Sir Maurice shook his head sadly over his mistakes with his son. "Does Lady Lucille make mention of the earl?" he asked cautiously.

"Only that he is in good health." Audacia glanced back at the first letter. "They saw him last week by these dates. I think I shall go walking, Father. Tell Miss Bea—" She halted and laughed at her mistake. "Tell Mrs. Ballin that I shan't be eating lunch."

"But, Audacia—"

"I am just not hungry now, Father. Perhaps I'll have a light collation with tea."

"Don't be too long in the sun," Sir Maurice admonished as she turned away.

Audacia walked back to him and kissed her father lightly on the cheek. "Truly, Father, all is well with me."

"I know how it is, Audee." He used her nickname of long ago. "I loved your mother dearly." Sir Maurice patted her shoulder awkwardly.

"It has been many years since you called me that." She swallowed the large lump in her throat that refused to go away.

"Only because I would give anything to have my carefree, raucous daughter singing and laughing about as in the past."

"Someday, Father . . . someday." Turning, she hurried from the workshop and out of the house and made for the trees and river in the distance.

" 'Tis a sin the way Miss Audacia pines for that man," Ballin muttered as he entered the workshop. "She went past me now almost in tears."

"That was my doing, Ballin," Sir Aderly dismissed the subject. "Did the gear arrive undamaged?"

"Aye, sir." He began to open the package. "I inspected it before I brought it along."

"Good, let's see it."

"Couldn't ye write to him, sir?" Ballin dared to ask. "Surely the man—"

"It is none of our doing. Meddling would only worsen

the pain for her. No, time will resolve it. Unpack the gear," Sir Maurice ordered with finality.

"Sir Aderly! Sir Aderly, come quickly. It's him." Mrs. Bea came flapping into the workroom.

"Calm yerself, woman," Ballin urged his wife. "Who has come."

"Him. You know, Lord Greydon," she finally managed the name.

Sir Aderly and Ballin exchanged glances. "See to the door," Aderly ordered. "I'll go to my office."

"Aye, sir—and wipe the grease from sir's face," the butler instructed his wife.

"Where is Miss Audacia?" Mrs. Bea clucked. "Of all times for her to be wandering off."

"It's probably best she is. If his coming is not on her account but only to see how his investment prospers she will be spared the pain of seeing him," Sir Maurice replied. "My cravat. I'll attend the grease, fetch my cravat," he ordered, "and my coat."

"That is not at all necessary," Lord Greydon's deep clear voice interrupted him. "It is a pleasure to see you again, Sir Aderly." He extended his hand in greeting.

Sir Maurice wiped his hands hurriedly on the cloth he held and shook hands, appraising the firm grip of the other. "You can see the experiments have not met with success thus far. We have not been as successful as one might wish," Aderly began.

"I am not here because of your work. May we speak privately?"

"Of course, my lord. My office is this way." Sir Aderly

motioned forward. "Ballin, Miss—Mrs. Ballin . . . please?" he looked at them impatiently.

Both started, then stepped aside and let the two men pass.

"I told ye all would be well," Ballin whispered, giving his wife a pinch.

"Mr. Ballin," Mrs. Bea protested.

"Does little good to complain ye don't enjoy it now. Experience tells me otherwise," he teased her.

Color surged to her cheeks. "Wait until we are alone, Mr. Ballin," she attempted a scold.

"Aye, I'll do that," he said and winked, "willingly."

Mrs. Bea reddened even more and waved a hand irritably as she walked away from him, a wide smile coming to her lips as soon as her back was to him.

"I heard that Mr. Ballin and Miss Strowne had married," Greydon commented as the two men entered Aderly's office.

"Yes, shortly after we returned home." Sir Maurice smiled. "We were pleased for both of them."

"You might wish to know Patrick Darby is on the continent now. I doubt he'll ever return. Lord and Lady Darby were able to keep a small portion of the estate when it was sold and do not lack for necessities."

"I had wondered about the outcome, and must thank you once again for dealing with the matter. Be seated. please." Aderly motioned to a chair across from his as he sat behind his desk. "Why have you come, Lord Greydon?" he asked, coming directly to the point.

"I wish to ask Audacia to marry me," the earl replied with equal bluntness.

"Do you have reason to think she is amenable to such an offer?"

"None, sir. I have come with little hope."

"Have you not thought she might consent because of gratitude?" Aderly questioned, watching him closely.

"The thought is not strange to me but I do not believe Audacia would do that. At least not without making it plain to me. She is not one to mince words." A wry smile came to his lips.

"How well I know that," Sir Maurice chuckled, then became serious once more. "On the occasion of Squire Webster's marriage to your sister one could not help noticing how aloof you held yourself from Audacia. I know that no letter in your hand has come here and she has written you none—is this not true?"

"Yes, sir." Greydon began to feel the urge to squirm under this father's questioning stare.

"For over two months no communication has been exchanged and yet you are here to offer for her hand in marriage? Is this not a strange way to pursue a courtship, my lord?"

Greydon coughed and cleared his throat. "I believe . . . believe . . . Well," he made a new attempt. "There was much I had to reason through before my mind was clear on the path I had to follow in this life. Audacia had made several points rather painfully clear and they had to be resolved before I felt free to come to her. Also, I believe that I have been the cause of some pain to her. It is not my desire to add to this. If you think it best, I will go now, without seeing her, and never attempt to do so again." The visage presented was impassive but the eyes and voice told of his pain and of the truth of his words.

251

"I believe you mean it, Lord Greydon. And respect you for it, whatever my thoughts have been on your behavior in regard to Audacia. That is between the two of you." He paused and rubbed his chin. "You do realize the tale of my wife's benefice to Audacia was greatly exaggerated? In truth, almost all is gone."

"I do. It is of no import."

"I know not what answer she shall give but I wish you the best of luck," Sir Aderly said, standing, a new twinkle in his eye. "If you've enough daring to want to brave life with my Audee, well, God bless."

"Thank you, Sir Aderly." Greydon pumped his hand enthusiastically. "When may I see her?"

"You can await her return—an hour or so hence, I would say."

"Is she out walking?"

"Yes, but suitably garbed this time." Sir Maurice winked. "I think you might know the spot she frequents. It is not far from the squire's gamekeeper's cottage, I'm told."

Greydon shook Aderly's hand with renewed vigor. "Thank you," he said again.

"Be off with you. What are you waiting for?" Aderly laughed and continued to chuckle as Greydon strode from the room and broke into a run as he left the house.

Sitting beneath the leafless tree beside the lazy river, Audacia reread Lady Lucille's letter. More had been said of Greydon than she had told her father and she now absorbed it word by word, even as she carried the memory of his cold, hard stance at the squire's wedding, aloof only to her. She had longed to reach out and touch him that

252

day, to offer comfort, and ached to be held and comforted by him. The few days she had remained in London with her father after the wedding had passed hope-filled for sight of him, for a note or word; but he had not appeared, none had come.

Audacia leaned her head against the barkless trunk and closed her eyes. Incident after incident flashed before her. Greydon proud, angry, teasing, amused, enigmatic. She slipped into a half-sleep filled with dreams.

Running steps carried Greydon well into the trees; as his destination neared, his pace slowed. He paused to pick a bouquet of purple heart's ease, their soft violet fragrance reminding him of Audacia.

Even hesitant steps take one to journey's end, and so Greydon arrived at the river. His heart fell as his eyes swept the empty area about him. It soared as he at last spied Audacia at the foot of the lifeless tree in gentle sleep.

Noiselessly he approached, drinking his fill of the raven locks, long enough now to curl softly about her neck. A silent oath filled him as he noted her thinness.

A step from her Greydon knelt on one knee and gently laid the bouquet of heart's ease in her lap.

At the sense of someone's nearness, she opened her eyes. "How lovely," she breathed dreamily as she took in the delicate beauty of the wildflowers. Cupping the violet blossoms in her hands, she breathed in their sweet fragrance. Slowly, her eyes looked further to the figure before her and she recognized Greydon. Several minutes passed as the two simply gazed as if to take their fill before the vision of the other could fade.

"Your beauty," Greydon spoke at last, "is as delicate,

as fair as this posy I offer. Only the flowers of the woodland can match your looks."

"It was you, then," Audacia said softly, "who sent the wildflowers to me. Why did you not acknowledge them?"

"I feared you would not wear them had you known their source," Greydon said, sitting beside her.

Audacia looked down at the blossoms scattered in her skirt. "You judged me too well. I was an overgrown child too filled with my own importance to see—"

"No," Greydon said, laying a finger across her lips. "This is not the Audacia I know." He looked at her closely as he removed it.

"I hope she is gone forever." A shadow of her former spirit crept into her words.

"My life would be oppressively dull if that is true." Greydon regarded her tenderly.

"You make fun of me, my lord?" she questioned, doubt and pain dulling her eyes.

"Am I to be drowned if I am guilty? Look, the river awaits me," he teased.

Doubt remained.

"My dearest Audacia, my love. Dare I hope you return some small part of the love I hold in my heart for you?"

A great joy began in the depths of her heart, it showed first in her eyes, then swept over her face.

Greydon crushed her to him, easing his hold only to allow their lips to meet. Long moments later, he drew back. "You forgive me?" he asked.

"Forgive you? You have done nothing. It is I who was ever rude and thankless." Audacia smiled and drew him to her hungrily.

"This shall never suit," Greydon said shakily some time

later and rose, holding out his hand to assist her. "Let us walk. Do not look so crushed, my love," he chided her. "I am but a man, and Geoffrey and Lucille do not return for two days more."

"What have they to do with us?" she questioned, taking his hand.

"If they are to be our witnesses, we must await their presence."

"Witnesses? But . . . ?"

"I have brought a special license with me . . ."

"So certain of me, were you?" Audacia tossed back saucily.

"I knew only that I dare not let you escape. Audacia, you will never know what a torture these past months have been. When the truth of your words finally sank through this thick-headed dolt—well, I cannot describe how I felt. No more than I can tell you the depth of my love for you."

"How glib my lord is," she tossed back, her former spirit quickly returning.

Greydon smiled widely. "I'll not be baited," he laughed. "But listen to what I have done. I know you shall be pleased. We have several factories—"

"My lord is also rich. Shall I value him more?"

"Listen to me, imp. I have arranged for amputees to be trained for what work they are capable of and offered them cottages and a small piece of land suitable for gardens. If this proves successful in a small way, then there are many who can be aided in this manner. And there are so many proposals I have in mind. My father is to introduce a bill in the next Parliament . . ."

"Parliament?"

255

"Yes, and I am going to try for a seat in the Commons. If I succeed . . ."

"Now my lord is too busy for his family, if indeed he has time to father one," Audacia noted in mock seriousness.

"In order to sire a family one must have a wife," Greydon returned in like vein.

A pensive frown came to Audacia's face and she peered solemnly around Greydon at the slowly flowing river.

"By the lord above," he expostulated, "what meaning am I to take from this?"

"Oh, I was merely wondering if the water was deep enough."

"This bodes ill for me." Greydon raised his eyes skyward.

"Drowning is not too mild a punishment for a gentleman who speaks of special licenses . . . love . . . and then launches into his plans for reform. Not that this lady is unwilling to listen; she is immensely pleased and proud by what he has done and means to do. Oh, yes." She nodded her head. "But a proposal of marriage would be much more suited to his earlier protestations.

"What should one do with such a dolt?" she teased.

Greydon cupped her face in his hands gently. "Marry him," he urged.

The response from Audacia as their lips met assured him she was willing to comply.